To Alison and Emily

Secret of Belle Meadow

Mary McVicker

Illustrated by Marcy Dunn Ramsey

TIDEWATER PUBLISHERS
Centreville, Maryland

LCCN 2003026812
ISBN 0-87033-554-5

Manufactured in the United States of America
First edition

CHAPTER ONE

Summer Ahead!

"I finally figured out what's going on," Karin said.

I was staring into my closet, trying to see how I could cram all of my clothes into half the space.

"What?" I said, not really listening.

"We might lose Belle Meadow," Karin said.

"What!" I hollered, turning around. Karin and I have been best friends for years, and Karin never says anything she doesn't mean.

"What did you say?" I asked again.

"I said we might lose Belle Meadow," Karin said in a flat tone of voice. She was looking out the window so I couldn't see her face. "You remember that hailstorm two years ago that killed everyone's crops. And last year when Mom was real sick, there were a lot of doctors' bills and things. At any rate, what with one thing and another, Dad had to borrow a lot of money. Now he has to pay the bank back, and he can't. If he doesn't start making payments this winter, I guess the bank's going to take Belle Meadow. *That's* what's going on."

"You've got to be wrong!" I said, but I had a sick feeling she wasn't.

"That's why Dad and Mom were talking about money all the time this spring and decided to take in boarders and turn Belle Meadow into a bed-and-breakfast this summer."

"The bank can't take Belle Meadow," I said, trying to sound positive.

"They took the Barrys' farm last year," Karin said, turning to look at me.

"But that was the Barrys," I said. "Everyone knows they were rotten farmers. Just look how Chris is in school! He's real lazy and always expects people to do things for him. Anyway, the bank can't take Belle Meadow. Your family's lived there for hundreds of years!"

The minute I said it I knew it was exactly the wrong thing to say. "Tina," I told myself, "Why don't you just bite your tongue off?"

Karin just looked away again and didn't say anything. I knew she was trying not to cry.

"This could be the year the crops are especially good," I said as hopefully as I could. That sounded pretty feeble, but it was the best I could think of on the spur of the moment. "You'll get lots of people to stay at your house, and you'll make plenty of money. You never know how things are going to turn out. That's what Mom always says, and look how things turned out for her when she got married again. Of course, it was a little confusing at first because Mom became

6

Mrs. Westcott while Steve and I were still Steve and Tina Mueller, but it all worked out."

"That's right," Karin said. "Just look. Now you get Anne coming to spend the summer, and you have to squash all your clothes to make room for her," Karin said.

"Well all right, I do get a boring stepsister for the summer. And I do have to share a room and my closet, but on the whole I think it's really good that Dad and Mom got married last year. I have too many clothes anyway. Or can you have too many, I wonder? There are many things I don't wear, and some—oh, never mind," I said. "Anyway, it'll be the same with Belle Meadow, I'm sure. Some things may look like setbacks—I think Anne is a giant setback but it's not her fault I suppose—but everything's going to turn out all right for Belle Meadow."

Karin didn't say anything; she just started looking through a pile of clothes on my bed. I tried to think of some idea for making a lot of money and saving Belle Meadow, but I couldn't come up with any ideas that didn't sound just plain dumb, so I went back to staring at my closet.

Finally Karin asked, "Have you decided what you're going to wear tomorrow?"

"No, have you?" I said.

"Mom said a skirt, so I was thinking of wearing my denim skirt and the white top that I usually wear with the red scarf. I want people to think I'm a professional waitress."

"Karin, you're thirteen," I said. "No one's going to think you're a professional waitress any more than they're going to think I'm a professional waitress. I just hope I don't drop a breakfast plate on anybody."

"At least with you working at Belle Meadow we'll get to see each other every day," Karin said. "Actually, it's kind of funny that both you and Steve are working there. I know Gary's pretty glad about it, because his best friend Bart lives clear on the other side of the county, and the two hardly ever see each other during the summer."

I shifted a handful of hangers to the empty half of the closet. "Jobs are so scarce around here this summer that if it weren't for Belle Meadow I don't think either of us would have a job. I know I wouldn't. Who's going to hire a thirteen-year-old except for babysitting—ugh! Seriously, though, it's a little scary to think of going to work tomorrow."

Karin nodded. "I'm sort of used to it because Mr. Neatherly and Miss Groton have been at Belle Meadow for over a week already. The first few days it was really odd having strangers in the house. Of course Miss Groton has lived around here ever since I could remember. You won't believe what a witch she is, by the way. But Mr. Neatherly's just here for the summer, so we didn't really know him. And tonight when the first bed-and-breakfast people arrive it's going to be *really* strange. Listen, we'd better hurry if we're going to figure out what to do about your closet. I have to be home in an hour to help with dinner."

"This is impossible," I declared. "I don't have room for everything as it is, and now I have to clear out half the closet and half the dresser for Anne. I know she has to put her stuff somewhere, but I really don't think it's fair. Thank goodness I'll be working at Belle Meadow most of the time and I won't have to entertain her."

"What's Anne going to do all summer?" Karin asked.

"I don't know. She's going to work at Dad's office three mornings a week, but aside from that, she's probably going to sit around and be dreary. Allingham, Virginia, isn't exactly Chicago, you know. Living here will be real different for her."

"I don't think it's going to be much fun for her," Karin said. "She doesn't know anyone. There's her dad, but you said she hasn't really lived with him for years. And she doesn't have any friends here. She met a few people last year when she was visiting, but that's not the same. You'll have to introduce her around."

"That's what Mom told me," I said. "I suppose I'll try, but you know there aren't many kids in town and there's nothing going on, especially this summer. Everyone's working on the farms. I'm never going to get to see Danny—not that I'd want to introduce him to Anne."

"I feel a little sorry for her," Karin said. "She's probably dreading this summer as much as you are."

"I feel a little sorry for her, too," I said, "except that she's so droopy."

"She is kind of quiet," Karin said.

"Droopy—and she's going to be here every single day, all summer, in this room, using this closet and that dresser. What am I going to do with all my stuff?"

"Start with what you're going to wear for work," Karin suggested. "You'll need skirts and tops for waiting tables and shorts and jeans for cleaning. I sure hope Mom and Dad's idea of turning Belle Meadow into a bed-and-breakfast and taking in lodgers works. So far it seems like a lot of work to me, but Mom says we can make good money at it if we work hard. I don't know if that's true, but I do know Mr. Neatherly and Miss Groton moved in last week and this weekend we're going to a movie for the first time in months. We used to go all the time. Still, I'm not crazy about having all these strangers living in my house. And don't forget I had to give up my room and move up to the attic—although I must admit I have a much bigger room up there."

"Well, I'm going to have someone who's practically a stranger in my room, using my closet and my dresser," I muttered.

"You'd better quit talking about it and start clearing things out," Karin said, "or I won't be able to help you. And if Anne's coming tomorrow you need to do it today."

"I know, I know," I said. I was taking a blue blouse out of the closet when I got my great idea. "I've got it! I'll clear a lot out and make my closet look really bare so Mom will think I need new clothes!"

"I think she'll know, but you've got the right idea," Karin said. "Are you going to put things in those under-the-bed storage boxes your mom got you?"

"Out of sight, out of mind, that's what my grandmother used to say. Maybe Mom'll forget I have all these clothes if she doesn't see them around."

"Fat chance," said Karin, "but anything's better than listening to you moan about Anne and having to share." She grabbed a denim shirt from the closet. "What about this?" she asked.

"Pack it. Pack everything," I said, gathering up blouses as fast as I could.

CHAPTER TWO

My Career Is Launched

I was excited about having a job and going to work until I actually had to do it. For one thing, I had to get up too early.

My brother Steve, who's fifteen, was also going to be working at Belle Meadow, helping Karin's dad and her brother Gary with the farmwork. It was Steve's first job too, and I could tell the minute I looked at him that first morning that I wasn't the only one who was wondering why on earth I was doing this.

Steve would be sixteen in October, but even if he could drive now, we'd still have to bike to Belle Meadow, because we only have one car in the family and Mom and Dad share that. I'd ridden my bike back and forth to Belle Meadow hundreds of times. It was an easy trip on back roads with hardly any hills, but I usually didn't do it at 6:30 in the morning.

I was tired. I hadn't slept very well. Right before I went to sleep I was thinking about what Karin had said about the bank taking Belle Meadow. All night in my dreams Karin and Gary and Mr. and Mrs. Martin were standing outside in a blizzard, huddled together in the snow, with a few pieces of broken-down furniture around them. In the bright morning sunlight the scene just seemed to be an illustration from the old set of Charles Dickens books downstairs in the living room, but in the middle of the night it seemed frightening and real.

While I was getting dressed I faced the situation. I had to do something, but the only thing I could do was to work hard at making the bed-and-breakfast a success and the boarders happy. Karin had said if her parents could make the interest payments on the loan, the bank wouldn't do anything for a while. Having the two boarders was a help, but a lot depended on the bed-and-breakfast. And since I was part of that business, a lot depended on me.

I realized something else. No matter what the job was called, I was going to be doing a lot of dishes and housework. Getting paid for cleaning would be a big improvement over doing the usual housework at home, but still, dust is dust. By the time Steve and I set off on our bikes, I wasn't feeling optimistic about anything.

Even at 6:30 we knew the day was going to be hot and humid. We were both sweating by the time we were two miles out of town. I didn't even want to think about pedaling back home in the afternoon sun.

We didn't talk much. We just pedaled at a steady rate down the narrow road.

When we rounded the last curve at the edge of the Belle Meadow property, I stopped. The air was heavy and still, and

I was a little out of breath. This was my favorite view of Belle Meadow with the house almost hidden by the giant trees. I couldn't see the river, but I knew it was there.

Belle Meadow was called a plantation but it was more like a farm. Sometimes tourists were disappointed because they expected to see a great huge house like you see in pictures, with lots of buildings and acres of fields.

The house was roomy, but it wasn't a mansion and it didn't have white pillars in front. It wasn't square like ours; instead, wings extended from each side of the main house. It had dormers on the front and wide porches on three sides. Just looking at it, a person would imagine this house had window seats and all kinds of nooks and crannies—maybe even secret places.

"At least you get to work inside where it's air-conditioned," Steve said.

I nodded. "Do you think it's going to be awful working outside all day?"

Steve didn't like the heat very much.

He shrugged. "Hard to say. I know Mr. Martin is pretty fair, and Gary says he doesn't mind if you take breaks, but . . ."

His voice trailed off. I knew he didn't want to admit to me that he was nervous.

"I know," I said, climbing back on my bike.

Steve just gave me a look, and I wondered if Gary had said anything to him about the money problems.

An hour and a half later I was in the kitchen, staring at a counter full of dirty dishes. "There's more to this bed-and-breakfast business than I thought," I said to myself. For one thing there were a lot more dishes. Karin brought in still another full tray.

At breakfast Karin and I had served while her mother cooked. Three guests—Mrs. Hughes and a couple whose name I kept forgetting—had arrived the night before. The couple was only staying overnight, but Mrs. Hughes was staying longer. She was an antiques dealer in Alexandria, and she was on what she called a "buying trip." She was going to visit dealers and people she thought might have pieces of furniture to sell.

She'd told Mrs. Martin she really liked this part of Virginia, and it was fun to explore "off the beaten path." She might stay for a week, maybe longer if she was successful in finding things for her business.

Having people stay for a long time wasn't the way most bed-and-breakfasts worked, but Mrs. Martin said, "Why not, if she's a good guest and interested in a long stay?" It made sense to me, especially since Mrs. Hughes seemed very nice.

You could tell Mrs. Hughes knew something about antiques because she was so interested in some of the furniture at Belle Meadow, especially the old game table in the living room. She'd already asked Mrs. Martin a lot of questions about the furniture and about families who'd lived in the area a long time.

With the two boarders (Miss Groton and Mr. Neatherly), Mrs. Hughes, the couple, Mr. Martin, Steve, and Gary, there were eight at breakfast. I wanted to be cheerful about all the business for Belle Meadow, but I was just tired. Everyone used an amazing number of dishes.

At least I hadn't dropped anyone's breakfast. And Miss Groton hadn't complained very much even though she changed her order twice.

Mr. Neatherly said "thank you" a lot but didn't talk much. Karin said he was always quiet. He even moved quietly, but that might have been because he was so small.

"He's probably always thinking about his research," Karin said. "He asks Dad and Mom a lot of questions about Belle Meadow or for directions to one of the other plantations or a library, but that's about all he says. He's usually gone during the day. He's like the other historians who have been here, except that he lives here too."

I finished loading the dishwasher and started wiping the counters.

"The dining room's done," Karin announced, coming back into the kitchen. "Mom says we should take a break before we start cleaning. Mrs. Hughes is going to Ashford Hill for the day, so we might as well wait until she's gone before we start on the upstairs rooms."

I helped myself to another piece of coffee cake and a glass of orange juice.

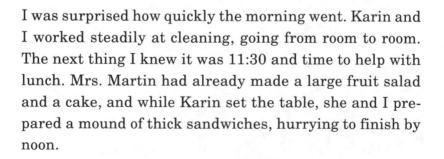

I was surprised how quickly the morning went. Karin and I worked steadily at cleaning, going from room to room. The next thing I knew it was 11:30 and time to help with lunch. Mrs. Martin had already made a large fruit salad and a cake, and while Karin set the table, she and I prepared a mound of thick sandwiches, hurrying to finish by noon.

Steve, Gary, and Mr. Martin came in right at noon; they washed quickly and sat down. Mr. Neatherly had been working on the porch most of the morning, so he and Miss Groton also came to lunch. As soon as we had everything on the table, we sat down too. I was pretty hungry myself, so I could imagine how Steve must have felt. I didn't get a chance to ask him how his morning had gone.

In half an hour almost all the food was gone, down to the last pickle. Everyone except Miss Groton helped carry plates and dishes to the kitchen. It was then that I got my first inkling of how much time I was going to spend preparing food. As soon as the kitchen was cleaned up, Mrs. Martin said, "We need to get the salads ready for dinner, and someone needs to snap the beans. There will be nine of us . . ."

Technically a bed-and-breakfast doesn't furnish dinner, but Mr. and Mrs. Martin decided it might attract more people if they did—at a price, of course. Since the nearest restaurant was miles away, offering dinner to people who were staying for several days made sense. Mrs. Martin told me they'd already gotten a number of reservations from people wanting to stay for several days, so I thought offering dinner was probably going to pay off.

I was supposed to help with some of the dinner preparations before I went home. That way Karin's mom could rest for part of the afternoon. On most days I was to leave by 2:00 or 2:30. Poor Steve had to work until 3:30 or 4:00.

By 2 o'clock we'd made huge bowls of cole slaw and potato salad. I didn't even want to guess how many boiled potatoes I'd peeled and chopped. Knowing I would also have to help with dinner when I got home was a depressing thought.

"I know you're anxious to get home and see Anne," Mrs. Martin said when we'd put the last bowl in the refrigerator.

Karin grinned at me behind her mother's back.

"Anne!" I said, suddenly remembering. Of course, Dad and Mom had picked her up at the airport in Richmond and were probably already home.

"We're done here," Mrs. Martin continued. "Everything went so well with you and Karin working. I really appreciate it! Be sure to write down your time."

"Yes. You're welcome, I mean, thanks," I stumbled, still thinking about Anne.

"Don't hurry in this heat," she added.

Karin walked out to my bike with me.

"You should have seen the look on your face when Mom mentioned Anne!" Karin laughed.

"I know," I said. "I forgot all about her."

"That was pretty obvious," Karin said.

On the way home I thought about Anne. I didn't want her to know how I felt about her staying with us, but I wasn't in the best mood. All I could think of was what a long and crummy summer it was going to be.

About two miles from home I decided I'd better get out of my rotten mood. So, while I pedaled and sweated I practiced smiling and telling Anne how glad I was that she would be spending the summer in Allingham with us.

By the time I turned into the driveway I sounded pretty phony.

CHAPTER THREE

Anne Arrives

Anne was taller than I remembered, and she was wearing her hair differently, shorter with wispy bangs. If I wore my hair like that I'd look like a turnip with a fringe, but it looked good on Anne.

She and Mom were in the kitchen having iced tea when I walked in. When I spotted boiled potatoes for potato salad cooling on the counter, I almost groaned.

"Hi, Anne," I said, as brightly as I could.

"Hello," she said back.

I poured myself a big glass of tea.

"Did you have a nice trip?" I asked politely. It was all I could think of to say.

"Yes, thanks," Anne said, just as politely. After a minute she asked, "How was work?"

"Fine," I said. "I'm working at Belle Meadow."

"That's what your mom said. We visited there last summer, didn't we?"

I nodded. "My best friend Karin lives there."

"I remember."

This was discouraging. Were we going to have awful conversations like that all summer? I was hot and tired, and the thought of having to make polite conversation all summer irritated me.

But suddenly I caught a hint of an expression on Anne's face, and it made me stop and think. I realized Anne hated this meeting and the planned summer as much as I did, and she was nervous. It seemed all wrong to me that someone should be nervous about my family and nervous about me. Mentally I took a deep breath and said, "I'm really glad you're going to be here this summer. I don't get to see my friends very much in the summertime, and it'll be neat to have a sister around."

Anne looked startled, then she smiled. This time it was a real smile. "I know it's a hassle for you having to share your room and everything," she said.

"Not really. Let's go upstairs and I'll help you unpack."

Mom stood up. "I'll be in the sewing room," she said. "I need to finish up that dress for Dorothy by Saturday."

Mom's sewing business is always extra busy in spring and the beginning of summer, with weddings and graduations and proms. Personally I can't imagine anyone liking to sew enough to make a business of it.

While Anne arranged her clothes I sat on the bed and told her about my job. "At least I'll get to see Karin a lot," I said. "Usually I hardly see any of my friends during the summer—which is one reason I don't like summer very much."

"Why don't you see them?" Anne asked. "Does everyone go away during the summer?"

"No, in fact hardly anyone takes a vacation because people can't leave their farms—that's a pretty blouse—almost all my friends live on farms or in the country. Everyone's scattered all over; it's not like Chicago where everybody lives together. Allingham's not very big and it doesn't have any good stores, so no one comes here to shop. About the only reason anyone comes into town is to go to the feed store or the library."

"I see my friends all the time in Chicago," Anne said. "Even if we don't live very close, I can just take a bus and see them. I can't imagine going all summer without seeing my friends—although I guess I will this summer."

"Do you mind?" I asked.

Anne shrugged her shoulders. "I guess not," she said.

She kept unpacking and I thought about what it must be like to be able to see your friends anytime you wanted. That part would be great, I decided, but I wasn't sure about living in a city with all those other people around me all the time. Living in a crowd would be hard to get used to. I supposed if you were used to living in a city like Anne was, though, living in the country might seem odd.

Anne even looked different from the kids around here. We both had the same sort of clothes, but hers looked different on her. Of course, she was taller and more pale with dark hair, while I was sort of beige and rounder looking. But that wasn't the difference. I remembered from her other visits that she even walked differently, quicker and more alert. She said it was because people who live in the city have to pay attention.

~◆~

Anne's mother must have given her one of those "make the best of it" lectures, because in two days Anne had settled in. She'd started her job at Dad's office, she'd met the neighbors, she'd gotten a library card, and she'd even lined up a babysitting job for the weekend.

She and Dad talked about the office and insurance a lot, and she talked baseball with Steve. Mom was going to teach her how to sew—I already knew, of course. Anne was still quiet and droopy around me, but at least she was busy and didn't just hang around like I was afraid she would.

"How can she be droopy and busy at the same time?" Karin asked me one morning when I was telling her about Anne.

"Beats me," I said, "but she is."

The Belle Meadow Bed-and-Breakfast was off to a great start. Mrs. Hughes's buying trip had been so successful she was talking about another visit toward the end of the summer "if it's not too much trouble."

"Not at all, we'd be delighted to have you," Mrs. Martin told her, and I could tell she was pleased.

Personally I thought it was a lot of trouble, but I had to admit Mrs. Hughes wouldn't be any more trouble than anyone else. In fact, Mrs. Hughes rescued me that morning.

When I'd brought Miss Groton her toast, she looked at it and announced, "This toast is too dark." The toast looked all right to me, but I said "sorry" and reached for the plate. I could feel my face turning hot, and I knew Steve and Gary were watching.

"Why don't you give it to me?" Mrs. Hughes said. "It's just the way I like it, and I'd hate to see it go to waste."

Miss Groton just sniffed and didn't say anything.

CHAPTER FOUR

The Oddest Day

The day started out just as usual.

By then—after five days—I felt like an old hand at the bed-and-breakfast business and I was even almost used to Anne staying with us. It always surprises me how quickly a person can get used to some changes.

I even liked riding to Belle Meadow with Steve early in the morning, before the heat got bad. Mornings were quiet and the air smelled good. Sometimes we talked, but a lot of the time we just rode along. Steve didn't say much about his job, and I think, like me, he had mixed feelings about all the work.

That morning while we were riding I was wondering what Miss Groton would find to complain about. She'd complained about something at breakfast every day, and I was wondering if she'd stick to breakfast complaints or move on to lunch. I had just decided she would stay with breakfast when Steve said, "I wouldn't like it if we lived in a place where people are always asking questions about where we live. Does Karin ever say anything about it?"

"About what?" I asked.

"Having people around the house all the time—Mr. Neatherly and Miss Groton. Yesterday afternoon when Gary and I were clearing part of the old cemetery, Mr. Neatherly just hung around and watched, asking questions and poking around. I know he's doing research on Belle Meadow, but he got on my nerves. I could tell even Gary was getting irritated, and he's used to having historians hanging around."

"At least Mr. Neatherly's quiet and polite," I said. "I'd rather have him hang around than Miss Groton."

"She's quiet," Steve said.

"Sure," I replied, "quiet and crabby!"

After Mrs. Martin, Karin, and I had breakfast, I took a cloth and the polish and began to dust downstairs. When I walked into the living room I almost tripped over Mrs. Hughes, who was on her hands and knees looking around the floor.

"I've lost an earring," she announced. "I think it must have fallen off when I was reading last night."

"I'll help you look for it," I said.

"Would you?" she asked. "In fact, if I don't leave right now I'm going to be late for my appointment this morning, and this particular dealer isn't the kind of person who understands someone being late."

"Sure," I said. "What does it look like?"

"It's just a thin silver loop," she said. "I'd really appreciate your help. I was sitting on the sofa by this table. I've already looked on the sofa and under the cushions, so it must have fallen on the floor. It might even have rolled under the sofa."

"I'll get a flashlight," I said.

She stood up and brushed her knees. "Thanks a million," she said.

I turned on the lamp, but there wasn't enough light to see the floor very well. So I asked Mrs. Martin for a flashlight and got down on my hands and knees and peered under the sofa. I wondered if Mrs. Martin knew about all the dust balls under the sofa, and it occurred to me I probably ought to clean under there. I shifted and shone the flashlight under the table in the corner.

The table had been in the Martin family forever. It was a very odd folding table. When it was closed, the top looked like a half circle. It opened up to make a full circle, and an extra leg slid out to support the second half of the table. When the table was open, you could see that it was an old game table; it was covered in a dark green material like felt.

My favorite part of the whole thing was a shallow drawer under part of the table. Mrs. Hughes told us that in the old days such a drawer would hold the cards and markers for the games.

I'd never looked underneath the table before, and I was surprised at how complicated it looked, with its maze of wood strips going every which way. But then I remembered how the table opened up to become a full circle and the extra wood supports made some sense. They would be needed to support the second half of the tabletop.

When I shone the light around under the table I could see a dull gleam against the far edge, almost hidden by one of the table legs. I was sure it must be the missing earring, so I crawled under the table to get a better look. There was quite a bit of room under the table in spite of the legs and support pieces. I'd never thought much about the underpart of a table, and I decided to see if I could figure out just how the thing worked.

I aimed the flashlight all around the top edge. It seemed odd that every detail of the underside of the table looked finished, although it wasn't as polished as the top surface. There were no rough edges, no unevenness anywhere. Whoever had built the table had been very caring about it, and I wondered who had put all that work into it, even finishing the parts no one would see.

While I sat there gazing around and wondering about this mysterious person, my eye was caught by a tiny uneven place in the wood, next to one of the leg supports. I thought the builder had made a mistake after all, although one tiny flaw on such a magnificent table, especially on the underside, wasn't bad. I ran my finger over the rough spot.

It wasn't rough at all, I realized. In fact, it felt like a tiny stick of wood about the size of a paper clip. I shone the flashlight on it and tried to get closer to look at it, but I bonked my head on one of the legs. I rubbed the rough spot a little, and in spite of the darkness and the grime, I could see a small stick of wood, like a patch. I poked at it.

The piece of wood moved, ever so slightly. I pushed at it again, and again it moved, very slightly. I pushed at it harder, and it moved again. Some grit fell on my face.

"What was it?" I wondered. Had I found something? But the table looked exactly the same underneath, and I couldn't even tell the piece of wood had moved. But it had.

I poked and prodded, but the piece of wood didn't move any farther. I decided it was just a patch that had worked loose, and I crawled out from under the table, feeling a little stiff.

The minute I stood up I realized I hadn't looked for the earring. I didn't want to crawl back under the table, so I decided just to pull it away from the wall and see if I could reach the earring—or whatever the shiny thing was—with a yardstick. The table was heavy, but pulling it out sounded better to me than crawling back under it and probably banging my head again. I grabbed the underside of the table and tugged. The edge moved with a slight upward movement, and I was a little startled until I remembered half of the tabletop was movable. That made sense until I realized I was pulling on the part of the table that should have stayed in place, not on the part that folded out.

I was really puzzled. I knew both halves weren't movable—or were they?

I carefully pulled on the edge of the table again. Slowly, and a little stiffly, it moved some more. I pulled again, and again it moved. I kept pulling—which was hard work—and the top of the table kept moving. I hoped I wasn't wrecking anything. I decided I'd better take the lamp off the table. Suddenly, the tabletop moved several inches, and I could see a shallow compartment.

How did the table work? I moved the top back to where it had been and crawled back under the table to move the little

piece of wood back to its original position. When I'd done that, I crawled back out and tried the tabletop again. This time it didn't move.

This meant the little piece of wood controlled the movement of the table leaf I thought was unmovable. I decided I needed to be sure, though, so once again I crawled back under the table and moved the piece of wood to its "open" position. Before I crawled out again I shone the flashlight on the underside of the table and very carefully looked for the shallow compartment. There was no sign of it. The table had a false bottom! I knocked against the wood to see if I could hear a hollow sound, but it sounded solid. I decided it wouldn't sound hollow because the wood was thick and solid and the compartment was very shallow.

I climbed back out so I could look at the compartment. I'd seen something in it, something that had looked like papers. I opened the compartment as carefully as I could.

They *were* papers, and they looked very old. They were dry and brittle, so I was very cautious about lifting them out. "How long had they been there?" I wondered.

I gently put the papers on a chair and tried to read the writing. The script was very hard to make out, but the papers looked like they were official papers or documents of some kind.

Under the final paper was a long thin book, very plain. It looked a little like an account book of some kind, but when I opened it I could see it wasn't an account book at all.

It was a diary.

CHAPTER FIVE

The Diary

A diary!

I was so excited I almost shrieked. I had to tell Karin right away! But I wanted to look at the diary first, so I sat down on the sofa and leafed through it.

The writing was small and old-fashioned, like the writing in the letters my mother has from her grandmother. But the writing was clear, and I could read most of it on the first try.

I skipped to the end of the book to see if the book said anything about who had written it. The last entry was dated during the American Revolution, over two hundred years ago! I couldn't believe I'd found anything that old. The writing in that entry was harder to read, as if it had been written in a great hurry. And when I finished reading the entry I knew I was right. Whoever had made the entry had written it in a tremendous rush.

"Wait until I tell Karin what this says!" I thought. I started to call to her when a noise in the hall made me stop.

Someone was in the hall, someone who was trying to be very quiet. The floor creaked, and I listened as hard as I could. Then footsteps crossed the hall, and I heard the outside door open and close. I thrust the small diary into the pocket of my shorts and ran into the hall.

If someone had been there a minute earlier, the hall was empty now. I couldn't see anyone on the porch, either. That puzzled me and I wondered if whoever had been in the hall was hiding. I ran across the hall to the dining room windows, but there was no one in sight. I almost ran outside, but I decided it was hopeless. With so many porches and doors, if someone wanted to come and go without being seen, they could.

I walked back into the living room and thought for a minute. The first thing to do, I decided, was to tell the Martins about the great discovery of the secret compartment and the papers in it. And the second thing to do was to keep my mouth shut about the diary and what it said until I'd had a chance to talk it over with Karin.

"Karin!" I called. "Mrs. Martin! Guess what!"

Karin came racing down the front stairs and almost ran into her mother, who was coming through the dining room.

"What is it?" they both said, almost at the same time.

"Look!" I blurted out. "A secret compartment, here in the table, and it has some papers in it! A secret compartment!"

"What!" Mrs. Martin exclaimed.

Karin's eyes got big. "A secret compartment!" she said, as if she didn't quite believe it.

I got excited all over again, just telling them about it.

"I didn't know there really were secret compartments, but look!" I opened and shut the compartment. "And it has old papers inside!"

"There's a lot of commotion in here," Miss Groton said in her most disapproving voice.

I hadn't even seen her walk in. "Look!" I just said. "A secret compartment, right here in the table!"

"Well my goodness!" Miss Groton exclaimed, and for once she didn't sound like she was complaining. "How did you find such a thing?"

"I never even knew it existed," Mrs. Martin said. "We've had the table all these years—it's been in Norm's family for hundreds of years, and nobody ever knew! Oh, someone obviously knew at some time since they put those papers in, but who knows how long that compartment's been forgotten? Karin, you must run and get your father right away, but tell him what happened so he doesn't think there's something wrong. He has to see this."

"These old pieces of furniture can be so interesting—may I look at the papers?" Mr. Neatherly asked. He'd come into the room after Karin and her mother, and he was walking around the table looking at the open compartment. "I've never seen anything like this table before. It's a wonderful piece."

"Yes, by all means look at the papers," Mrs. Martin said. "I've always been very fond of this table just as it was, but now I like it all the more. Why haven't we found the compartment before?"

Everyone looked at me. I explained all about being under the table and the little piece of wood and the leaf moving.

Then Mrs. Martin wanted to look under the table and see for herself how the little piece of wood worked as a release mechanism for the secret compartment. When she stood up, Mr. Neatherly wanted to look.

I was under the table this whole time, wedged against the back legs. Mr. Neatherly took such a long time, I was feeling very cramped from crouching so long. I was relieved when he finally stood up and I could crawl out.

I was just standing up when Miss Groton said, "I think I'd like to see it too," and to my great surprise she sort of whisked herself under the table. "Now where is that catch?" she asked in her thin voice, and I had to kneel down yet again and show her.

Then Mr. Martin and Steve and Gary came into the house with a great clatter.

"What's all this about a secret compartment?" Mr. Martin asked. "Karin said something about some papers?"

"They look like old receipts and orders," Mr. Neatherly said. He was standing at the end of the room looking down at the papers spread out on the sofa. "They're very old, from around the time of the Revolution."

I nodded to myself, remembering the diary in my pocket. Thank goodness it was such a small book, or it never would have stayed hidden while I conducted tours of the underside of the table. I was starting to think I had a good future in the tour business!

And sure enough, Mr. Martin said, "Let me see how this works."

After everyone had tried the wooden catch and moved the tabletop and opened the hidden compartment, I explained again about looking for the earring and trying to move the table. "I thought I'd broken it somehow when it moved," I said.

After a long time everyone finally drifted away and went back to what they'd been doing. Mr. Neatherly took the papers up to his room to examine them, and Miss Groton went back to writing letters on the side porch. Karin started to walk toward the stairs, but when I saw everyone else had left I motioned Karin back into the living room.

"There's more," I whispered.

"A treasure?" Karin whispered back excitedly.

"Not exactly," I told her. "Look, we should have some time after lunch before I go home to talk about this."

Karin looked at me for a minute and didn't say anything. Then she nodded. "We'll go down by the river. Mom won't care as long as the cleaning and the lunch and dinner stuff are finished."

We always went down to the river when we had something important to talk about, unless it was raining or it was wintertime. In hot weather the riverbank was shady and there was always a slight breeze. Best of all, though, it was private, and with all the people at Belle Meadow these days, that was important.

The rest of the morning dragged. I finished my cleaning—retrieved the lost earring—and helped make a huge chef's salad and biscuits for lunch.

By 1:30 we'd finished and we were crossing the meadow on our way to the river. I knew what people meant when they talked about something "burning a hole in your pocket" because that's exactly how the diary felt. I kept expecting someone to say, "What are you doing with that book in your pocket?" and once when Miss Groton called out "Tina!" I jumped a foot. She only wanted me to ask my mom something about the next meeting of the library group they both belong to. I must have looked guilty, because I sure felt guilty.

When Karin and I finally sat down at our spot, the one under the biggest magnolia tree, Karin turned to me. "What's up?"

"This," I said, fishing in my pocket for the diary. I had to stand up to get it out of my pocket, so my announcement wasn't as dramatic as I'd pictured.

Karin looked through the book, then looked at me. "A diary?" she asked.

I nodded. "Not just a diary—look at the last page. It's from the Revolution," I added.

As Karin read through the tiny script, her expression got more and more serious. When she finished, she started to read it again.

"Read it out loud," I said.

Karin cleared her throat and began.

We may have to flee soon. The family has been so active and our reputation is such that should the British reach Belle Meadow I fear the consequences. For safety we have buried the jewelry and silver and only the two of us know where it is. This is a grave risk, but I fear for the secret if more are told of it—I have not told Louise. We will have to take the chance that one of us will be left alive to reclaim the treasure. May the whispering bough that has sheltered us so often now protect our property. As I write this, I see it from my window. May God be with us.

For a long time Karin looked straight ahead and didn't say anything. Finally she spoke, her voice very quiet and serious. "Tina, there's a treasure buried at Belle Meadow! And we've got to find it!"

"Do you think it's still here after all these years?" I asked. I'd been asking myself that same question over and over since I'd read that part of the diary.

"It could be," Karin said. "People are always finding stuff hidden away. Look at what they found just a few months ago at that place near Williamsburg."

"That's right! And didn't someone find a lost music manuscript by Mozart or somebody?"

"Exactly," Karin said. "Of course the treasure might not be there . . ."

"It might not," I agreed.

"We don't want to get our hopes up." Karin's always so sensible.

"No, we don't," I agreed. "But what if it is? It's possible, you know."

"It's possible," Karin said. Then she turned to me with a determined expression and said, "Let's do it. Let's not tell anyone and let's find whatever's there."

It was exactly what I'd hoped she'd say, of course, and I grinned. "Of course we can do it!"

"We have to be careful," she said.

"Careful."

"We need to figure out a plan."

We both thought for a minute.

"Have you ever heard anything about anyone finding something buried at Belle Meadow?" I asked.

"A long time ago an archaeologist dug a test pit near where the old house used to be," Karin said.

"The old house?" I asked.

"You know, in the meadow."

I shook my head. "You'd better tell me again. I don't remember exactly."

"The old house, the real Belle Meadow, was by the river in the meadow we just cut through. It burned down over a hundred years ago, so the family just moved to the house we're living in. In the old days that was the overseer's house."

"Overseers had nice houses," I commented.

"It used to be smaller, but someone built extra rooms and the porches in the early 1900s," Karin said. "I don't think the overseers lived *that* well."

"OK, now tell me about the archaeologist and the test pit, whatever that is," I said.

"That's where they dig down to see if anything was buried there. I don't remember much about it, except that I got to watch them dig, and they were real nice."

"Did they find anything?"

"Mostly rubbish and tiny pieces from old junk. They seemed to think it was pretty neat, but it didn't look like much to me. They certainly didn't find any silver or anything like that. And I've never heard of anything else. There are so many old stories about Belle Meadow that I'm sure I would have heard something, or Dad would have. I'll ask him."

"Would the Historical Society have anything?" I asked.

"They might," Karin said. "They have a lot of Belle Meadow stuff. But then again they might not have anything useful for us. We need to look. How on earth are we going to figure out where the treasure is buried?"

"It's buried under a tree," I said.

Karin and I looked around. There were trees everywhere we looked, and off to our right we could see a thick woods. "Tina," Karin said, "there are about eight thousand trees at Belle Meadow."

"That's a little discouraging," I admitted. "But at least we know it's under a sheltering bough."

Karin just gave me a sour look.

"I know," I said, "we have to figure out something else."

"Are there any other clues in the diary?" Karin asked.

"I don't know," I said. "We don't even know who wrote it, though I think it was probably a man—it does say 'I have not told Louise.' There isn't anything after the part about the treasure, which makes me think he didn't come back. Wouldn't he have kept on with his diary?"

"I think he would," Karin said. "Why didn't he take it with him?"

"Maybe he was afraid someone would find it or he'd lose it, and he knew it would be safe in the table. Or maybe he had to flee so quickly he didn't have a chance to get it," I suggested.

We read a little more in the diary, but the earlier part of the book wasn't nearly as interesting. And although we talked most of the afternoon, we didn't come up with any ideas. Finally I told Karin I needed to get home.

"You should take the diary home with you," she said.

"Why?" I asked, surprised.

"I just think it's safer with you," she said. "I'm not sure why."

I thought about someone spying on me and sneaking across the hall and out the door.

"All right," I said, standing up.

I could hardly wait to get home and tell Mom about the secret compartment, and I rode much faster than I usually did in the afternoon. All the way home I kept thinking "Is it possible?" until the phrase made sort of a rhythm that I pedaled to.

"Is it *possible, is* it *possible . . ."* all the way home.

CHAPTER SIX

Real History

Mom's always great when I tell her news, and even Anne got excited when I told them.

"You found a secret compartment!" Anne said, her eyes big. "How exciting! How did you find it?"

I went over the whole story again (minus the diary, of course) and when I finished Mom went right to the telephone and called Mrs. Martin.

"Marie!" she said, "Tina's just told us the most amazing thing! Imagine finding a secret compartment in that lovely old table! Would it be all right if we came to see it?"

We all drove out to Belle Meadow right after dinner, even Steve. He said he wanted to see the table again.

I didn't even mind having to climb under the table and demonstrate again how I found the compartment, even though I banged my shoulder.

Mrs. Hughes was fascinated with the secret compartment. "I've seen a number of old game tables," she said, "but never one like this." She kept circling the table, which had been moved to the center of the room so it could be seen more easily. Every so often she'd stop and run her hand over the top of the table and shake her head.

When everyone had seen the compartment and tried it out, we all sat out on one of the porches and drank lemonade and ate popcorn.

Mom asked Mr. Martin about the papers.

"They're mostly letters talking about political activities," he said, "but one is from a relative, apparently in answer to an earlier letter. I don't think the letters are valuable, but they might be interesting from a historical standpoint. What do you think, John?" Mr. Martin turned to Mr. Neatherly.

"I can't really say whether or not the letters are valuable," he said. "Certainly what they say about political activities on a local level is very interesting."

"I thought this area was your specialty," Miss Groton cut in.

"Not exactly," Mr. Neatherly said, looking very serious. "I'm interested in that time period, but my primary area of interest is daily life, how people managed day-to-day during the Revolution."

"I see," said Miss Groton, and she gave a sniff.

Mr. Neatherly looked satisfied.

"He sure hasn't learned anything about Miss Groton," I thought. When she gives a sniff like that she's unhappy about something.

"Are you going to have someone look at the letters in case they're more valuable than they appear?" Dad asked.

Mr. Martin thought a minute. "I suppose we'll have someone from the Historical Society examine them. At some point they'll probably go to the society so they're with the rest of the Belle Meadow documents and papers."

"Does the Historical Society have a lot of other things from Belle Meadow?" I asked.

"Oh yes, they've made quite a collection over the years. None of it's particularly valuable, but it says a lot about a smaller plantation in this part of the state."

"What do they have?" Anne asked.

"Mostly household items, a few letters, things like that."

"Is there any way to find out who hid the papers in the table?" Karin asked.

"I don't know if you could find out exactly, but you could make a guess," Mr. Martin said. "In fact, what might be interesting would be to look in the wills and inventories and see if the table is mentioned."

Karin looked puzzled, so he explained.

"You know that a will tells how property is passed on to people after someone dies," he said.

Karin nodded.

"When that happens, a listing is made of what property is in that person's estate—it's called an inventory of the estate. Some of the old wills and inventories go into a lot of detail about what the person owned. You might look to see if the table is mentioned in any of those old documents."

I thought it sounded terrific. "Where would we find those?"

"Wills and inventories are at the courthouse in Kingston."

"Can we go sometime?" Karin asked. I held my breath.

"I have an idea," Mom said. "I need to go to Kingston in the next few days to buy some material and do some shopping. If it doesn't interfere with your work, you can come."

Mrs. Martin nodded. "It's fine with me," she said.

I couldn't tell if that meant Karin could come too, but I didn't want to ask.

"It's lucky for us the Historical Society takes such an interest in Belle Meadow," Mr. Martin said. "It's an unusual property and we really don't have time to look after that part of it. We're too busy just living here."

"Why is Belle Meadow so unusual?" Anne asked. "Is it because it's so old?"

"Partly its age, and partly its size. Many of the older plantations that have survived were the much larger major plantations. They're the ones people always hear of."

Anne nodded. "We visited some last summer."

"There were many farms that were quite small, too, of course. But many of the middle-sized plantations haven't survived, and historians want to know more about property that size. And much of Belle Meadow is intact. It has always been exactly the same size it is now, except for some erosion along the river. Of course the fire destroyed a lot so the collection isn't as complete as it might be, and the original house is gone. But apparently there's enough here to keep a historian busy now and then."

He nodded to Mr. Neatherly, who smiled and gave a slight bow.

"When was the fire?" I asked.

"During the War of 1812," Mr. Martin said.

"Just like the White House!" I said. We'd studied the War of 1812 just this past year.

"Not exactly. The British didn't burn Belle Meadow. What probably happened—although I don't know for sure— was a chimney caught fire and the house burned. That wasn't uncommon in those days."

"If the main house hadn't burned, we'd have a lot more information about the plantation," Mrs. Martin said. "As it is we're lucky as much survived as did. By that time the family had expanded, and part of the family was living in the over-seer's house, which is our house now. Many of the family's things were in the overseer's house and escaped the fire in the main house."

"Like the table?" Karin asked.

"Yes," said Mrs. Martin. "It must have been in the over-seer's house."

"Do you know anything about the main house?" Anne asked.

"Not very much," Mr. Martin answered. "There is one small sketch, but you can't tell too much from it. We know the house was in the meadow on the rise overlooking the river. You can guess about where the house stood. Some ar-chaeologists paced it out several summers ago and made a rough map. I'll try to find it for you."

"Why didn't someone find the compartment before?" Steve asked.

"Who knows?" Mr. Martin said. "I suppose nobody ever knocked the table or pulled on the leaf just right."

"I'm really intrigued with that compartment," Mrs. Hughes said. "I know I'm repeating myself, but in all my years in antiques, I've never seen anything quite like it. Some of the old rolltop desks have hidden drawers, but I've never seen one in a game table. And this isn't exactly a drawer, either."

I was intrigued, too, but for different reasons. "Would the table have been made at Belle Meadow?" I asked. I knew people made a lot of their own furniture back then.

"It might have," Mr. Martin said. "I don't know if there was a woodworker at Belle Meadow. That compartment raises a lot of interesting questions."

"And you don't know the half of it," I added to myself, not daring to look at Karin.

CHAPTER SEVEN

Soggy Day, Soggy Outlook

The rain woke me up early Thursday morning. At first the rain sounded good to me, because it's been dry for a while, and I knew Mr. Martin was worried about the corn being too dry.

Then I remembered about riding my bike to Belle Meadow and back in the rain. I knew Dad wanted the car because on Monday he'd told Mom he planned to set up some appointments in the west part of the county, and what day wouldn't she need the car? Naturally it turned out to be the day it was raining. Even if Steve and I did get a ride *to* work, someone would have to come and get us. We couldn't just arrive for work and say, "Hello, here we are, by the way can someone give us a ride home this afternoon?" At least my backpack was waterproof—I'd packed my skirt inside.

Anne was still sleeping. She doesn't know how lucky she is to live in Chicago, where she can take a bus or a train and go somewhere without having to ask someone to take her or trying to decide if it's too far to bike. I like living in the country—or to be precise in a small town in the country—but there are definitely drawbacks.

At least it wasn't pouring. The rain was slow and steady. I've never been to the jungle, but sometimes when it rains here in the summer I know something about what a jungle feels like. It's hard even to breathe.

"That's all the more reason not to go to work today," I thought, but I could hear Mom downstairs, and I knew if I didn't get up on time she'd be cross. At least I wouldn't have to work tomorrow, since we were going to Kingston.

Steve and I rode slowly. The rain had eased up, and it was too hot and humid to hurry.

"What are you going to do today?" I asked when we had crossed North Creek, our halfway point. "Are you going to work outside in the rain?"

After a minute or so he said, "I guess so," and he sounded so miserable that I decided I'd better not complain, at least not out loud.

"I think having you help is really making a difference," I said, trying to cheer him up.

He didn't say anything.

"And you're probably making it easier for Gary, because he doesn't think he has to do it all himself," I added.

"I suppose it does go better with two instead of just one," he said finally, "like you and Karin."

"I hadn't thought of that," I said.

"Or you and Anne," he added.

I definitely hadn't considered that. We all had chores to do around the house. That was how it always had been. Dad had died when we were little, and Mom had to work a lot just to keep us going. Anne joined right in and helped without making a big deal of it.

"She's all right," Steve said. "How's it going?"

"Fair," I said. "She's nice enough and that helps."

"It can't be much fun for her, having to live with us. She hardly knows us, and she doesn't have any friends here," Steve said. "Summer's not exactly party time around here."

"No kidding," I said. It already seemed like weeks since school had let out and I'd seen my friends, especially Danny. But that was summer, and it could be depressing if you thought about it too much, which I didn't want to do.

I decided to think about what I might change my name to. I've had it with Tina.

If I were short and cute that would be one thing, but I'm not cute. Mostly I'd like to have a more elegant name. Anne is a nice name. It sounds royal.

I'd just made up my mind to be Alexandra when we arrived at Belle Meadow, soggy but on time. The dampness was more from sweating under our rain gear than from the rain itself. I dried off and changed quickly, and we started our breakfast routine.

"How are you at fixing things?" Mr. Martin asked Steve when everyone sat down.

"Not bad at some things," he said.

"He's pretty good at fixing stuff," I said, setting down a big platter of pancakes. "Mr. Belden, our neighbor, showed him how to do all kinds of repairs."

Steve turned red and shrugged. "Well, someone has to know how to do it," he said, with a slight glare at me.

"There are a number of projects piling up in the barn and tool house," said Mr. Martin. "No better time to do it than a rainy day. It'll go fast with three of us."

The day dragged. I was thinking about the diary and about going to the courthouse to look up people's wills and things. Mom had said we might go the next day. The courthouse wasn't open on Saturday, and anyway, there were several guests coming for the weekend and Mrs. Martin had asked me to work on Saturday. Anne was going to come along to Kingston with us, and she and Mom were going to shop and pick out material while I was at the courthouse.

That reminded me about Mrs. Albright and the twins coming to see Mom after lunch. I hoped they'd be gone by the time I got home. I didn't mind Mrs. Albright but the twins were pests, and I usually got stuck watching them. Mrs. Albright's youngest sister was getting married, and the twins were going to be flower girls. Mom was making their dresses. Their mother would probably go for the angelic look, which would be completely out of character, but then in a way everybody wears costumes in a wedding.

Still, making clothes for weddings helped keep Mom in business, and there had been a lot of years before she remarried when the business had been even more important than it was now.

Maybe it was the rain getting on everyone's nerves. Mrs. Hughes was supposed to go to an outdoor antique show about forty miles away, but it had been postponed because of the rain, so she was, as she said, "at loose ends."

Mr. Neatherly, on the other hand, was very busy. He'd brought down some of his books and had spread them out on a table on the north porch, and he was reading and making notes. Every now and then he'd stop and write.

I was keeping a good eye on both of them.

Miss Groton was keeping an eye on me, I suppose to see if I was doing the work I was supposed to. Once she said something about me "lollygagging around," and suggested if I was tired I should probably get to bed earlier. I hoped she wasn't going to complain about me to Mrs. Martin. I knew I really wasn't working as hard as I usually did.

I was glad when the rain stopped and the clouds began breaking late in the morning. It looked like Steve and I were going to get lucky.

The Albrights were still at the house when I got home at 2:30. Mrs. Albright and Mom were talking about patterns and material, trying to make sense of a sketch her sister had sent, supposedly showing how the twins should look as flower girls. (Mom said later it was a terrible design, one that would be difficult to make.) And Mrs. Albright is the kind of person who always waits until the last minute to ask Mom to do something. I know she doesn't want the twins to outgrow whatever Mom makes for them, but doesn't she know how much work it is for Mom to make those fussy clothes she always picks out?

I went upstairs to change, because the ride home had been really sweaty. Anne was at Dad's office. Usually she just worked in the morning, but Mrs. McNair had a dentist appointment and some errands to do after lunch. Dad had several appointments, and he needed Anne to answer the phone.

The twins were having a grand time. Mom had pulled out some scraps of cloth so they could "make" doll clothes, since they'd brought their favorite stuffed toys and a doll. Unfortunately, they'd seen her take the scraps from the closet where she kept a lot of the good material, and when Mom and Mrs. Albright had gone into the living room to talk about patterns, the twins had pulled out all the material from the lower shelves, and they were playing among the crumpled heaps of cloth. At least they were too short to reach all the shelves, I thought. As it was, they'd created a real disaster.

"You shouldn't have done this," I said. "Mom gave you plenty to play with." I didn't care that I shouldn't speak that way to a client's children. Someone had to. I sat them on the window seat with their dolls and toys and scraps and started picking up and folding the material.

A minute later Mom and Mrs. Albright came in from the living room. I could tell Mom was angry when she saw what had happened. Mrs. Albright just said, "Oh, look what those rascals have done!" as if it was a great thing they'd made such a mess, and of course the little girls just smiled sweetly.

I just kept folding material and stacking it neatly while Mrs. Albright kept talking to Mom and the twins kept playing with their toys and the scraps of material. I thought they'd never leave.

"At least they didn't get into the really good stuff," I told Mom when Mrs. Albright finally left and was driving down the street. "It doesn't look like they damaged anything or got it dirty."

"Thank you, Tina," Mom said, "I appreciate your help. That woman!"

We were just finishing when Anne came in. I have to say the closet looked great, with everything neatly folded and stacked.

Mom told her what had happened. "I suppose it was good for me to go through everything," she said. "I do forget just what material I have. But I like to choose when I do something like that. That woman!" she said again. "How did work go?" she asked Anne.

"I think all right. There were a lot of phone calls, people calling with questions. Insurance is certainly complicated. I just wrote everything down for Dad. And someone wanted directions but got annoyed when I couldn't help them. They were coming from some town I'd never heard of. I asked if Dad could call him, or if he could call back, but he sounded real huffy about it and just said no. I told Dad when he got back. I hope he didn't mind."

"I'm sure he didn't," Mom assured her. "Let's have some iced tea."

"Thanks Mrs . . . Mom."

Mom looked at her for a minute. "You know, we need to figure out what you call me. You can't simply not call me anything all summer, and Mrs. Westcott just won't do."

Anne got very red. "I'm sorry," she said.

"It's nothing to be sorry about. We just have to figure out something you're comfortable with. Mrs. Mom is an interesting sort of compromise, but together, I think we can come up with something better." She put her arm around Anne's shoulder and they walked out into the kitchen.

I figured I was better out of this, and anyway all day I'd been thinking of reading the diary again. I thought there

might be something else in it about the house or the land, something that might give a clue about what the writer had been thinking. When Anne and Mom decided to have some iced tea on the porch "to recover," I went upstairs.

I'd been keeping the diary in a large envelope under my mattress. I don't think that was the best place, but I couldn't think of anywhere else. I pulled it out, made myself comfortable against my pillow, and began to read.

The room was warm, and I began to drift a little bit. I wasn't really dozing; I was trying to picture how life must have been at Belle Meadow so long ago, and I wondered who all lived there, and if there was a girl my age.

"I thought . . ."

I grabbed the diary and tried to shove it under the mattress, but I couldn't get it back under because I was on the mattress.

"You don't have to hide things from me."

I looked up. Anne's face was very white, with red splotches on her cheeks. I'd never seen her look like that, and her voice was very quiet and shaky. That was the worst part, her voice. It wouldn't have been quite so awful if she'd yelled.

"I know you didn't want me to come and you don't like me," she continued, and she sounded horribly sad and defeated. "That's all right, I guess. But I'm not a sneaky person and I don't snoop. You don't have to hide things from me."

"I don't hide things from you! Listen . . ."

But she was already running down the stairs, and I heard the back door slam.

CHAPTER EIGHT

Unraveling

I put the diary away and ran down the stairs.

All I could think of was how hurt and upset Anne was, and all because of me. I told myself she shouldn't have misunderstood so badly and jumped to the conclusion I was trying to hide the diary from her. But I felt sick inside. I hated that things I'd done and said had hurt someone so much. It was a grand mess and I didn't have a clue what to do about it. But I knew I had to do something.

I had to go after her and explain.

I thought she might be sitting out in the back garden on the bench that's hidden from the house by some bushes. She goes there sometimes, I think when she wants to be alone. But the garden was empty when I got there, and I ran back to the house.

Mom was standing inside the door.

"I assume you're going to straighten this out," she said sharply.

"Oh, Mom," I said, almost crying, "it's such a big mess. Anne misunderstood and now she's—where is she? I've just got to explain."

"Probably at her dad's office."

For once I didn't even care if Mom was angry. All I cared about was how hurt and unhappy Anne was, and I knew it was my doing.

I was panting and sweating and out of breath when I got to the office. Outside the door I took a deep breath. I opened the door.

Mrs. McNair was at the computer. She looked a little surprised to see me, not because I didn't come to Dad's office now and then, but I suspect I didn't look so good.

"Is Anne here?" I gasped.

"Yes," she said, smiling. "She's in with her dad."

I looked at the door to his office.

"Why don't you catch your breath for a minute and have a drink of water?"

I nodded and sat down, and she brought me some water.

A minute later I stood up and walked into Dad's office.

"Hello," I said, feeling stupid.

"Hello," he said.

Anne just looked away, but I could see she'd been crying.

I plunged right in. "Look, Anne, I know you're upset and mad at me and hurt and I don't blame you, but it's not what you think. It's a terrible misunderstanding. You've got to let me explain."

She didn't say anything.

"Please. Give me five minutes and promise you'll listen. Then if you're still mad at me that's all right. Well it's not all right, but at least you'll be mad at me for the right reasons. Please, Anne."

After a long minute she sniffed and said, "All right."

And she turned to face me.

"Take your time," Dad said, as he got up to leave.

I hardly knew how to start.

"It's a big misunderstanding. The book you saw me hiding is a diary I found with the papers in the secret compartment of the Martins' table. It tells where there's a treasure buried at Belle Meadow, and Karin and I want to find it."

This wasn't right. The real problem was that I was trying to hide it.

"We've been keeping it secret because we think everyone will just laugh at us. But what's worse is we think someone else is after the treasure."

"So you're hiding it from everyone?" Anne said.

"Yes, I'm worried about it. Someone was spying on me when I found the diary, and we're afraid whoever it is knows something and is after the treasure. So when you came into the room I wasn't really hiding it from you, I was just hiding it without thinking about it. And I don't think you're a sneak or snoopy. I'm scared someone else is going to get the treasure. I'm scared the Martins are going to lose Belle Meadow."

Anne didn't say anything for a minute. I waited, worried, but I couldn't think of anything else to say.

"I knew there was a problem," she finally said, "but I didn't know it was so serious."

I nodded.

"Do you really think the treasure is still there?" she asked.

"I don't know," I said. "I hope so. I think if someone had found it a long time ago there would be stories about it. But someone might have found it and not said anything—stolen it maybe. I really don't know what to think."

She thought a bit. "But what about all that stuff you're hiding in boxes under your bed? Every now and then you go rummaging in them when you think no one's looking."

For a minute I couldn't think what she was talking about. Then I remembered.

"Oh! Those are my clothes! They used to be in the closet. Actually you're right, I am sort of hiding them from Mom. I thought if she saw how bare my side of the closet is she'd think I needed new clothes. Of course she bought the boxes, but I hoped she might forget about that. So far it hasn't worked. I think I might as well put some of them back. But there's a lot of stuff that doesn't fit any more, and I haven't sorted them out. I could use some new clothes, but Mom never believes me when I say that. I wonder if she's seen my half of the closet."

All of a sudden Anne started laughing. "Tina, you're a mess!"

"I know," I said, and I laughed too, because she wasn't being insulting or mean when she said it.

When we stopped I said, "There's more. You're really mistaken about one thing. I like you, and I like having you here. It's nice to have someone to talk to. The other night I had a nightmare and woke up, and it was good to know you were across the room."

She stood up. "Thanks." For a minute she looked out the window.

I thought I hadn't done a very good job of explaining things or making them better, so I was relieved when she turned around and said, "Maybe I could help you sort out your clothes so you don't have to go crawling under your bed every time you need to get dressed."

"I'd like that," I said. "And maybe you could read the diary and see what you think."

CHAPTER NINE

Family Trees

"How long do trees live around here?"

Kingston is only about a half hour ride, but it seemed long. I kept thinking about Anne's question. I'd told her that some trees were hundreds of years old, and some are, but the question bothered me. I had to admit that the chances of *the* tree still being alive might not be good.

Anne had come back home with me. Mom was in the kitchen fixing dinner. She looked up when we came in the back door, but I guess she figured we'd worked it out, because she didn't say anything, and we went upstairs.

I started pulling the boxes out from under my bed, and Anne read the diary. After I took a good look at some of the clothes, I went downstairs for one of those large trash bags that we use when we're taking something to the church charities. I was going to make a good contribution. Some of those clothes had been around for years, and they were way too small for me.

Anne read carefully, and once or twice she went back and read something again. I kept watching her out of the corner of my eye, trying to see what she thought about it. After she finished reading the diary—it didn't take very long once you got the hang of the writing—she stared out the window for a long time. Finally she turned to me and asked about the trees.

I'd thought of that, of course. So had Karin. Figuring out which tree was going to be tough enough; the whole thing was hopeless if the tree wasn't there anymore.

"You're right," she said finally. "You've got to try to find it. You can't just give up because it might not work out. You'll always wonder if you could have found it. Well, let's get at these clothes, and then we need to figure out a better place to hide the diary. Under the mattress is too obvious."

She had a great idea for a hiding place. It took some time to arrange, but I didn't think anyone would ever find it. All the time we just talked about what we were doing and the diary, as if nothing had happened, but at the same time some of the conversation had an uncertain feel to it, as if we weren't sure the other person knew the language.

After dinner we went back upstairs and she sat on her bed watching me fold clothes and put them in the bag. When I was about done she asked, "Do you have a map? I can't picture the layout of Belle Meadow."

"I tried to make one, but it came out pretty messy," I said. "I'll show it to you. Can you draw?"

We worked on the map for about an hour. It's hard to explain to someone how a map of a place should look, and I wasn't sure about distances between things. But I could see if I'd asked her to put something in the wrong place. Fortunately she had a good eraser and a lot of patience. Neither of us said anything about the blowup that afternoon. I wondered if it would ever come up again.

~~<><>~~

By the time we were halfway to Kingston, I was beginning to wonder what in the world I thought I was doing going to the courthouse to look up wills and stuff, like I was a grown-up. Mom had called to be sure it was all right and to inquire if someone could help me if I had any questions. She'd liked the woman she'd talked to.

"Mrs. Estes said it would be fine if you came to do some research. She said she'd be glad to answer any questions about Belle Meadow. I told her you're a good student and you're helping Mrs. Martin this summer."

"Did you tell her I'm not twenty-one yet?" I asked.

"I told her you are thirteen."

"I'm surprised she said I could come," I said.

"So was I," Mom admitted. "I thought if there was a problem we could do the research together. I'm probably old enough," and she laughed. "To tell the truth I suspect her office is pretty quiet at times. There probably aren't a lot of people looking up old land records, and she may get bored."

Earlier in the week going to the courthouse had sounded like a good idea, almost an adventure. Now that we were actually on our way to Kingston I wasn't sure. I didn't even know just what I was looking for. What was I going to say when Mrs. Estes asked me what I wanted to find out? I couldn't say, "Where the treasure's buried."

I thought about all the different people who had lived at Belle Meadow since the treasure was buried. All those people, all those names.

"I bet I find a lot of good names," I said. "Maybe I'll get an idea for a name for me."

Mom sort of hunched her shoulders. "Are you still thinking of changing your name?" she asked. "There's nothing wrong with the name Christina."

"I know."

"It's a good name."

I recognized that tone of voice. And suddenly it dawned on me that she and my real dad had picked out the name for me, and maybe Mom felt bad when I said I wanted to change it. In my most grown-up voice I said, "Yes, it *is* a good name," and I sat up straight to look older.

"Anyway," I thought, "I can always add a secret middle name to go with Christina Jean Mueller." I still liked Alexandra, but when I said the whole thing together it did seem like a lot of syllables.

"I didn't know Karin's name is spelled with 'i-n.' Isn't it usually 'e-n'? K-a-r-e-n?" Anne asked.

"She's named after a great aunt," I said.

"Maybe you'll find her today," Anne said.

"Unfortunately, no," Mom said. "It's her mother's family, not her father's."

Mom and Anne started talking. I quit paying attention and looked out the window. We were coming to one of my favorite places on the way to Kingston, a really old farm that had been deserted for years. It was kind of sad to see the fallen-down buildings, except for some reason wildflowers grew like crazy all over the old farmyard. "Probably good manure over the years," I thought.

I pointed it out to Anne, who thought it looked sort of romantic "like something you'd see in a painting."

We were quiet then, and all of a sudden it came to me.

"White oak!" I blurted out.

"What?" Anne said.

"White oak!"

"What about white oak?" Mom asked.

"Anne was wondering if trees lived for hundreds of years around here; she's sort of interested in botany. I just remembered a white oak tree can live for hundreds of years. It can, can't it?"

"Of course," Mom said. "And remember when we went to Mount Vernon last year, there were trees George Washington had planted. And I think there are some at Monticello that Jefferson planted as well. I hope we can get to Monticello this summer, Anne. It's such an interesting place, especially if you're interested in botany. The gardens are lovely, and you know Jefferson experimented with growing all kinds of plants no one had ever grown here."

"It is a neat place," I agreed.

Anne turned around and looked at me. "Botany?" she mouthed.

I just shrugged and smiled.

"The high school here has a very good botany teacher," Mom continued. That's the thing about Mom, once she gets hold of an idea she doesn't let go easily, especially if it involves doing something for someone else, in this case encouraging Anne's supposed interest in botany. I could only hope Anne didn't mind. Who knows, she might actually like botany!

Mom was still talking. "Not every school has botany courses, but because this is such an agricultural region, there are plenty of students to take it. Most of all, though, he makes it very interesting."

"My school is a little too much city for botany, I guess," Anne said.

After that no one said anything until we got to the courthouse.

Mrs. Estes was one of those very tall, thin women who look a little on the grim side. But once she started talking I could tell she was much nicer than that.

"It's very nice of you to let Tina look at the records," Mom told her, talking the way grown-ups do as if you weren't really in the same room.

Anne was looking at some old maps on the wall. I held my notebook and pen and tried to look responsible.

"The old records are the most interesting," Mrs. Estes said. "People sometimes put all sorts of comments and information in them, not like today where everything is written according to the formula. And I've always thought Belle Meadow is such a nice piece of property. Several years ago the Martins let the County Historical Society tour Belle Meadow—it was most interesting. You're working for the Martins this summer?" she said to me.

I told her about the bed-and-breakfast. "It's nice to have something to do during the summer," she said. "When I was growing up I always thought summers could get long with everyone working on the farms. It seemed like I never got to see my friends."

"Karin's my best friend, too," I said. "This way I see her almost every day."

"Now, tell me what you'd like to look at," she said. "Just what are you looking for?"

"I'm not sure," I said, "but there's this table at Belle Meadow. It's a rather odd table, and I found it had a secret compartment. One of the people staying there this summer knows a lot about antiques. She sort of buys and sells them. She said the table was very unusual, and we were wondering about it. Someone said it might have been mentioned in a will or inventory, which might give us some idea about how old it is. There were some papers in the compartment that were from around the Revolution."

"That's a very good idea," Mrs. Estes said. "And who knows if someone may have said something specific about the table? I made sure I'd have plenty of time for you this morning, so you can ask any questions you want."

Yes, she was a nice lady.

Mom said she'd see me at the lunchroom at noon, Anne wished me luck, and they left.

"Why don't you come behind the counter and I'll show you where the records are kept?" Mrs. Estes asked, and led the way. She opened a door that seemed to have a lot of locks on it, and we went into a room with shelves of books on one side of the room and more shelves with files and folders of papers on the other walls. The books were different sizes, some tall and skinny, some shorter and thicker. Most of them had dark brown covers.

"Are these the records?" I asked. I'm not sure what I expected records would look like, but I hadn't pictured all these books. "I guess some of these are pretty old."

"They are," she told me. "And dusty, too. I learned early to wear dark-colored blouses to work!"

"There are a lot of records here," I said. It never occurred to me just how much space records take up.

"We go back quite far in this part of the country," she said proudly. "Our records are very complete, also. Luckily the courthouse never burned, even during the Civil War. A lot of courthouses have very incomplete records."

The old books had a musty smell, and the place felt dusty, although it was clean. "It's a good thing I don't have allergies," I thought, remembering Sarah who usually sat behind me in classes and always had a cold, except it was allergies.

Mrs. Estes took one of the books down from the shelf and put it on a table. I noticed there were many small tables scattered around. "You don't want to have to carry these far," she said, opening the book.

It was from the late 1700s, but the ink looked surprisingly clear. "The paper was better in those days," she said. "Of course the ink faded, but not as much as you might think. Were the papers you found very faded?"

"No," I said. I hadn't thought about it very much, and I decided to look at the paper in the diary more closely when I went home.

"You probably know this, but when someone dies with a will, the will is filed with the court. The court decides if it's a valid will, and if so, the will provides the directions for settling the estate."

"Are there very many will arguments?" I asked, not sure what to call them.

She laughed. "Not as many you might think from watching television, but more than there should be. People can be awfully careless about their wills. They're not clear about what they intend, or they don't make out their wills properly—the court is very precise about how wills should be written. And sometimes some of the heirs simply don't like the will, so they try to figure out a way to have it invalidated. Unfortunately, because family members are usually involved, those fights can be terrible. Sometimes they split a family."

It sounded like a plot for a good movie to me.

"The court pays attention to how the property is distributed to the heirs, to be sure everything is done according to what the will says. One of the first things the executor does—that's the person in charge of the estate—is to list everything in the estate. That's the inventory. The older ones can be very interesting. People listed things we take for granted today, but back then furniture and possessions were more scarce. Even household implements and tools were listed."

I was beginning to wonder how I was going to manage this. "How many wills are related to Belle Meadow?" I asked.

"Quite a good number," she said. "But the ones you want to look at are probably going to be just the ones the owners left. That's where the table would be mentioned, I would think. If not, we'll look at other wills."

"How am I going to know which ones to look at?"

"Technically, you'd have to trace the owners. You start with the present owners and go back."

I made a face.

"Don't worry. I have a list of the owners. The Martins gave a list to the Historical Society about five years ago—I can't remember why, but it may have had something to do with the archaeologists. I have a copy. I went ahead and pulled out the books and files with the wills and inventories I think you'll want to see."

"Oh!" I said, relieved. "Thank you!"

"I knew you needed to get your project done today. I'll help you look, if you like, or if you run short of time."

She was either very nice or very bored to do all this, I thought.

"Do you want to start with the Revolution, or start at the present and go back?" she asked.

"Could I see the list of owners?" I asked.

And there it was. Alfred Martin owned Belle Meadow during the Revolution. He must have been the one who wrote the diary!

"Can I copy this list?" I asked. Karin must have forgotten about their list, I thought. But it hadn't occurred to me to ask, either.

"I'll make a copy for you."

But then, while she was making a photocopy, I thought maybe it wasn't Alfred who wrote the diary. Couldn't someone else have written it? Maybe Alfred was off fighting. Maybe he was with George Washington! I liked that idea—it was like knowing someone who knew George Washington.

Maybe Alfred's wife had written the diary. She would have been the one left behind to take care of things while he was off with the troops. A lot of women were left to run the farms and even the businesses.

Anyone could have written it—a cousin or one of Alfred's children might have been old enough.

Then I thought, why did it matter? Did it change anything for Karin and Anne and me looking for the treasure? It didn't really. But even so I liked to think it was Alfred.

Alfred's will was hard to read and didn't say anything about the treasure or even the table. In fact, it didn't say much of anything at all, and the inventory was just as disappointing.

The next owner was Alfred Charles Martin, and then there was Charles Alfred and another Charles.

"Do the names ever get confusing?" I asked Mrs. Estes.

She just laughed. "I'll say! It's not so bad for the property records—you can usually keep them straight, but it drives the genealogists crazy. We get a lot of people looking for their ancestors, making their family trees, you know. Back then there was a real tendency to use only a few names many times all through the family. If you went back in your family you'd probably find that too."

I wrote down Charles Martin and opened the file with the next set of papers, carefully putting down the date. I'd looked ahead on the list of owners and there weren't very many different names—I knew I'd really mess up if I didn't make careful notes.

"I don't think that's changed much," she continued, "not really. In the 1800s you see repeat names in many families. And it still continues today. I'm named after one of my aunts, Emmeline. My mother shortened it to Emily, fortunately. Maybe you're named after someone."

I shook my head. "I don't think so. Mom would have mentioned it, and we've been talking about names a lot lately. But I think my brother Steve is named after one of my father's cousins."

I don't know much about my father's family. They lived far away, and Dad died so many years ago. I thought I might ask Mom, but I'm never sure about bringing these things up with her.

"Back to work, Tina," I told myself. "Think about that later."

I was trying not to get discouraged, but I have to admit I'd hoped for some good information. I knew I wouldn't find a treasure map or anything like that, but I thought I might find something! All the talking and looking was taking a long time, and it was getting closer to the time when I was supposed to meet Anne and Mom. I knew I'd have only a short time after lunch.

And there it was. Not exactly a treasure map, and not anything about the treasure. In fact, that had me curious. None of the wills or the sketchy inventories (when they existed) had mentioned anything about silver or jewelry and money—which I would think would be the treasure. Nothing.

But Charles Martin did say something. "To Albert, my oldest living son, the game table, with the reminder of the family legend that it must never pass out of the family."

"Wow!" I said, without thinking.

"Did you find something?" Mrs. Estes asked. She was working on some papers of her own.

"Listen to this!" And I read the sentence to her.

"Oh, that's great! He specifically mentions the table you're interested in! And a family legend—how mysterious. It must have meant something very special to the family! Does he say anything more?" she asked.

"I don't think so," I said. "He mentions a few other pieces of furniture but it's not like he lists the whole house."

"Let me see if there's an inventory," and she went rummaging through another file.

"No, but those records are very incomplete. If property stayed in the family people often didn't bother with an inventory, even though they should have. It was just another bother, I suppose."

The name changed the next generation—there was only one son, and he was killed in the Civil War. The daughter married someone named Graham—but the Alfreds, Alberts, and Charleses still kept showing up, although not as regularly. The owners changed more frequently then, but at least Belle Meadow was never sold. Our history teacher had told us those were hard times. I knew a lot of the farms in the area had been sold and often the families had gone west to start over.

Several owners later the name changed back to Martin. Another daughter had married a cousin and she had inherited the place. Belle Meadow seemed to have had bad luck with sons. I remembered there were a bunch of Grahams in the graveyard and their tombstones were dated well past the time of the name change.

I wondered if all the Charleses and Alfreds and Alberts were in the cemetery. It would be interesting to look them up.

All those people. And at least one of them had known the secret we were trying so hard to figure out.

CHAPTER TEN

Finding Traces

When it was time to go to lunch Mrs. Estes said, "You don't have that much more to do. I think the two of us could finish in an hour with no problem."

"That would be nice," I said. "I'd hate to leave without finishing. I don't know when Mom will be coming back to Kingston, and if she does it might be a day when there are a lot of people at Belle Meadow and I'd need to help Mrs. Martin."

She nodded. "We'll see if we can't finish up."

"Oh, thank you!" I said. "And thanks for all your help this morning!"

She just smiled. "You're welcome. I enjoyed it too. And I'm glad you found that bit about the table!"

I felt so good about my morning I sort of floated down the street to the lunchroom, or I would have if it weren't so humid. We were definitely getting into the hot part of the summer. My shirt was sticking to me by the time I walked in the door, right on time. Anne and Mom came in a few minutes later.

"Where are all the packages?" I asked. "I thought you were going to buy tons of material and trimmings and things."

"We did!" Anne said, and I could tell they'd had a good morning as well.

"I already know what I'm going to order," I announced when we sat down in the booth.

"That's because you always order the same thing!" Mom said. "So do I, for that matter."

The lunchroom—that's what everyone called it even though it had another name and served breakfast as well—was known for its specialty, Virginia ham on cheese biscuits. Of course you can get those a lot of places around here, but for some reason the lunchroom's are the best. I think it's the biscuits. Mom always ordered chicken salad, and I have to admit it was pretty good too, with nice fruit in it. We always shared—she gave me some of her salad, and I gave her half a ham biscuit.

"Get something different if you like," Mom said to Anne, "and you can try ours. Then the next time we come you'll know if that's what you want."

But she had the ham biscuits too.

"Tell us about your morning," Mom said. "What did you find?"

"First of all, everyone has the same names, or some combination of those names. If Mrs. Estes hadn't written out the names of the owners and the dates for me it would be very confusing. And she even pulled out some of the files to get me a head start, and she's going to help me finish up, too. She says the two of us can finish in an hour easily. Is that all right? If I go back for a while after lunch, I mean? Or I could eat fast and you two could take your time."

"Don't worry about it," Mom said, with a laugh. "You should never rush ham biscuits. Have you found anything?"

"Yes," I said, "someone actually mentioned the table!" And I read them the statement in Charles's will that I had copied down because I knew I wouldn't remember it exactly.

"How interesting," Mom remarked. "The table must have been considered very important."

"I think it was," I said.

"Maybe one of their ancestors had made it," Anne remarked, which I thought was very smart of her to say, because, really, if you didn't know about the diary the statement didn't make any sense.

"That could be," Mom agreed.

"Some of the wills and inventories are interesting," I said, "even though they don't have anything I'm looking for. Mrs. Estes says people sometimes put all kinds of things in the old wills."

"It sounds like she's being very helpful," Mom said.

"Oh, she is," I said. "She's one of those people who gets interested in what you're interested in, like Miss Wessels at the library."

I never quite figured out just what Mom and Anne had done all morning, but they'd had a good time at whatever it was, so I was glad.

"Anne has a good eye for fabrics and color," Mom said. "She came up with something for Mrs. Albright's dress to give it a nice look, a little different. She—Mrs. Albright—has a tendency to dress a bit little-girlish herself, you know, and I'm trying to steer her toward a different look to give her some style. Anne spotted some fabric with a very subtle pattern in it, and she came up with the idea of making it into a more simple looking dress, almost on the order of the A-lines that used to be so popular. We found a wonderful pattern. I think it's going to be stunning."

Anne had turned bright red.

"That's great, Mom," I said. "You can use some reinforcement with Mrs. Albright."

"Oh, I don't know about that," Anne said. "Now the twins, though, that's where anyone could use reinforcement!"

"The same goes for treasure hunting, too," I thought. "When's the wedding?" I asked.

"Not for several weeks," Mom said.

"Lots of time," I said. "For you, that is, not me."

"Still, I wish she'd give me more time on these things."

I guessed they'd done some other shopping as well. "I got you another top for the bed-and-breakfast," Mom said. "Anne got a new shorts outfit."

"Anything for you?" I asked.

"That's after lunch," Mom said.

"I hope you find something! Anne, Mom's notorious for not liking to buy herself anything. She always says she could make it better, and she probably could, but then she never sews for herself."

"I'll do my best to encourage her to look," Anne said.

"Something different," I suggested. "Maybe in a pretty lilac."

"We'll see," Mom said, the standard answer.

I was glad she and Anne were having a good time together, and I thought it must make Anne feel a little better about being with us.

I asked Mom if I could be excused a little early; I wanted to have enough time to finish. I didn't really expect to find anything more, but it seemed important to look at everything, just in case. I knew Karin would ask, because she's a real stickler for finishing everything.

Mrs. Estes and I went through the last names carefully but didn't find anything interesting or helpful. Although I wasn't expecting much, it was a letdown after the morning. By 2:00 I was sitting on the steps in front of the courthouse waiting for Mom and Anne to drive up. They weren't coming until about 2:15, but I was glad to be outside in spite of the heat. "Poor Mrs. Estes, with all those dusty books and records and files," I thought.

I kept thinking about Anne and how pleased she'd looked at lunch when Mom told me she had a good eye for color and design. I wondered if her mom ever said nice things to her, and for some reason I had the impression she didn't. I liked the fact that she and Steve were talking more now too, real conversations, not just made-up things to be polite. And Anne was making friends with Kathy Norlin who lived on the other side of Allingham. They'd gone to the movies with Steve and some of his friends several days ago.

I thought about how hard it would be to go live with strangers, except for her dad, and try to get along all summer, especially since she was shy—and I almost fell off the step. Shy? Was Anne shy?

"Of course she is, you dummy," I told myself. How had I missed it? I think if it had been me I'd have cried myself to sleep every night.

Maybe she did when she first came. Maybe she still does.

"I'm going to drop off you girls and take this right to Mrs. Albright," Mom said when I got into the back seat. "If you want to see the fabrics and trims, they're in the bags beside you, Tina."

The material for the twins' dresses was light pink, and there were yards of a beautiful ribbon in the bag as well. I didn't know how Mom was going to use the ribbon, but that was her problem. I didn't have to pretend to like what Anne had found. The material for Mrs. Albright's dress was very light beige with a hint of pink, not exactly shiny, but like chrome that doesn't glisten. The pattern was very subtle.

"She's actually going to look good in this!" I said.

"She is an attractive woman," Mom said, "if only she'd quit picking out those styles that look like what the twins would wear. I hope she likes this."

We were supposed to make the meat loaf for dinner before Mom came back. "Use the recipe in my file," she said. "It's the one I always use. I know it seems a little hot for meat loaf, but Steve really works up an appetite, and we can't have salad every night. We're having corn on the cob with it, so if you get a chance, would you husk about ten ears?"

Anne and I walked down the driveway to the back door. "I'll make some iced tea," Anne said as we went into the house. "That should be good with dinner, too. Or do you ..."

I never found out what the "or" was. She stopped short, staring at the floor. I bumped into her, said "sorry," and then I stared too.

There were footprints on the floor, traces of big muddy footprints, leading from the back door up to the entrance to the living room.

CHAPTER ELEVEN

The Nerve!

Even though no footprints were on the stairs, we rushed for our room, never thinking for a minute of anything but the diary. I was angry. Imagine someone coming into our house like that for something that didn't belong to him—or it could be a her, come to think of it. It didn't occur to me it could be anything else, like a thief or someone wanting to do harm.

Someone had been in our room—no doubt about that. Whoever it was hadn't messed it up, but if you were looking for signs of someone having gone through things, they were there. I always close drawers, and several of them weren't quite closed. The beds were a little rumpled and I knew very well someone had run their hands under the mattresses.

Anne opened the closet door and felt under the shelf. "It's still there!" she said.

"I knew it would be!" I said. "No one would ever look there."

The hiding place had been Anne's brilliant idea. We'd painted a big envelope dark brown. Then we'd put the diary in it and taped it to the underside of the closet shelf, back in a corner above the hanger rack. We'd even painted the tape. Unless you knew it was there, you'd never just spot it.

"What are we going to do?" she asked.

I knew what she meant. Should we tell Mom and Dad? If it were a real thief we'd have called the police already. But we thought this wasn't a "real" thief at all. He—or she—wanted only to steal the diary and find the treasure.

"Let's see if anything else is disturbed," I said. We looked carefully through the house. Just as we thought, the person hadn't bothered anything else.

"How'd he get in?" Anne asked.

"Just walked in I suppose," I said. "The nerve!"

"Oh, right. This is Allingham. I'll never get used to leaving doors unlocked."

"We don't always," I said a little defensively. "But there are always windows open, too."

"You know," Anne said, "it must have been someone who knew we'd be gone today," Anne said.

I stared at her. Of course, that made sense. The thief had come from Belle Meadow, and everyone on the place knew we were going to Kingston today.

"But who?" she said.

And that was the question.

"Maybe it wasn't someone from Belle Meadow," Anne said. "Someone in town could figure out the house would be empty for a while. Since they knew what they were after and where to look, they didn't need a lot of time."

We talked about it for a while, but didn't get anywhere. It occurred to me we'd better get busy fixing dinner—and mopping the floor. At least the thief had taken off the boots so only the kitchen floor was muddy.

"I think we should just clean up the footprints and not say anything," I said.

"I don't know . . ."

"I know, it isn't right. We really ought to report it. But I think it'll just get everyone all upset, wondering what's going on. Isn't it going to look a little odd that the person just concentrated on our room?"

Anne shook her head. "You're right. It's all wrong, you know, but you're right."

"I'll start on the meat loaf if you'll mop the floor," I said. "Or I'll mop and you start cooking."

"No, that's fine. This won't take long."

I looked at the clock. We should have plenty of time to get everything done, or almost done, before Mom comes home, I decided. But just in case I husked a few ears of corn so it would look like we were well along on everything.

Steve came in right after Anne finished the floor. "Careful, the floor's a little damp," she told him. "We tracked some mud in and don't want your mom to know."

"No problem," he said, and went upstairs to shower.

We really raced around and had everything ready and the table set when Mom came home. Dad arrived a few minutes later. Neither Anne nor I felt really comfortable about not telling them about the intruder.

Everyone said the meat loaf tasted great. It's funny how feeling guilty can change the taste of food you really like.

CHAPTER TWELVE

Discovering the
Old Belle Meadow

After doing my research in Kingston, going back to work the next morning was a letdown. The only thing I was looking forward to was telling Karin all about what I'd found.

I had made copies of my notes so I could tell her everything exactly. And, of course, I couldn't wait to tell her about the intruder.

Anne wasn't enthusiastic about going to work this morning either. "I know I'm helping, and some of the work is interesting, especially when I'm using the computer. I know it's important for me to learn to do everything so I can take care of the office when Mrs. McNair goes on vacation in August. But I don't want to go to work today," she told me.

I agreed. It had been a real shock to me that "the working life" wasn't all it was cracked up to be. I liked getting my paychecks on Saturday, but there was still a lot of dusting and dishwashing to do before summer would be over. Even the ride to work seemed especially long that morning.

"Someone broke into our house!" I whispered to Karin the first chance I got. "Nobody knows except Anne and me!"

"What!" she said.

"I'll explain later," I said, because her mom was coming into the kitchen.

When Karin, Mrs. Martin, and I were having our breakfast, Mrs. Martin asked me about the trip to Kingston. For one awful moment I thought, "She knows!" Then I realized that of course she thought I was going just to see about the table.

I told her how nice Mrs. Estes was and how I liked looking at the old wills. I didn't say anything about that curious statement in Charles's will about the table, although there really wasn't any reason to keep it secret. I felt less deceitful when I remembered anyone could look up the records and see the will.

Still, I was glad Miss Groton wasn't around, because she'd somehow know I wasn't telling everything. Miss Groton was a person who always knew such things. Fortunately she'd taken her crocheting out on the north porch, explaining at length about her niece's new baby. I didn't know if the baby had happened or was about to happen, and I didn't ask.

Fewer guests at Belle Meadow meant less money for the Martins, but at least Karin and I had an easier cleaning schedule for a few days, which gave us more time to talk.

"Did you find anything?" she asked the first chance she got. "And tell me all about the intruder!"

"Yes and no," I said. "I found some really interesting things, but I still don't know where the you-know-what is. And there isn't much to tell about the intruder except he didn't find the diary, thanks to Anne's brilliant idea for hiding it."

Karin listened intently while I told her what I'd found. "That's wonderful," she said when I finished telling her about the family legend. "It shows we're on the right track!"

I thought about that for a minute, and then I said, "No it doesn't. We already know we're on the right track because we've already found the diary. So it doesn't tell us anything at all."

"I guess not," she said, "unless there's something else in the table."

I shook my head. "I don't think so. I think the diary was it. Not that the diary isn't plenty—in fact, that's the point. The diary is a real important thing, and that's why there was the family legend about the table. Anyway, everyone has examined the table very carefully by now, and there can't be anything else in there . . . unless there's another secret compartment."

Karin and I looked at each other, then ran to the living room.

"Let's measure it," Karin said. "We can tell if there's some other space that's not accounted for."

In the last mystery I'd read, the girl had found a secret room that way. It sounded like a good idea to me, except I wondered how you could miss an entire room in a house. The room was pretty big, too, not like a closet, which I suppose you could overlook.

"Do you think there's a secret room here?" I asked Karin.

She shook her head. "I don't see how. I read the same book, remember, and I thought of that too. But all the rooms here are square. Years ago when people added closets they used the end of one room; half of the space became a closet for that room, and the other half a closet for the room next to it. All the space is accounted for—I checked. But another secret compartment might be a different thing."

Karin draws better than I do, so I measured the table and she drew the diagram. When we were done we had a neat picture of the table, but it told us nothing. There was a lot of space not taken up by the compartment, but we had no way of telling if some of the space was another compartment, or if it was just the underpart of the table. I knocked under the table, but I already knew that effort was hopeless. The table was solid; even the compartment we knew about didn't sound hollow.

"We aren't getting anywhere," I said. I was getting discouraged. "What we really need to do is figure out just where the old house stood and what the plantation looked like. Then we could figure out where Alfred's study was."

"Of course!" Karin said. "Then we'd know what he was looking at when he looked out his window."

"That was Anne's idea," I admitted. "When you gave her the map the archaeologists had drawn for your dad, she copied all the details onto her map."

"We'll go right after lunch. I guess we'd better get started on the upstairs rooms," Karin said.

I had just finished mopping the wood floor in Mrs. Hughes's room when I noticed the dirt on the closet floor. I almost dropped the mop. I looked in the closet and saw her boots, caked with dirt. Not only that, but the dirt was still slightly damp.

Could Mrs. Hughes have broken into our house? I didn't know what to think. That just didn't sound right, but there were the boots. And that dirt hadn't been there a few days ago when I'd mopped the floor.

Now, she could have been walking in the woods, or she could have worn the boots on one of her exploring trips to an old plantation. She goes into the backcountry a lot. It's easy to get muddy walking around there, because a lot of people didn't really have walks. Or, a person could get mud on their boots walking through someone's garden, sneaking up to their house. She knew we were going to Kingston.

I went into Miss Groton's room where Karin was fiddling with a bunch of thimbles. Miss Groton fussed if we didn't leave them in a certain way after we dusted. We never got it right.

"Karin," I said, "Could you come here a minute?"

She just shook her head when I showed her the boots.

"I don't know. I have to say that Mrs. Hughes is awfully snoopy, and she keeps hanging around the table. I think I told you she was snooping in my room one day."

I nodded.

"Just because we kind of like her doesn't mean she couldn't have gone into your house looking for the diary. I'm not sure why, though. Do you think she saw you take the diary out of the compartment?" Karin asked.

"She might have," I said. "I'm pretty sure someone did."

We didn't talk much the rest of the morning; I think we both felt we had a lot to think over and we were a little broody.

After lunch we went to the meadow.

"This is the area where Dad's map showed the old house stood," Karin said, waving her arm around. "The archaeologists walked it off with him years ago when they were digging the test pits."

"I see it on the map," I said, peering at the lines on the paper. "Look, there's where the old road would have come up to the front of the house."

"And it makes sense," Karin said. "If you were building a house near the river, this is where you'd build it."

I had to agree. The meadow is a slight rise, not quite high enough to be called a hill, and it slopes gently down to the river. The rise is flat at the top and makes a wide rectangle, slightly angled to the river. It's a space made-to-order for a medium-sized plantation house.

The location also makes sense because at that point the river, which isn't very wide, makes a gentle turn and forms a natural baylike area.

"Can't you just picture the boats docking down there and people coming up to the house?" I asked Karin.

She nodded. "And imagine doing almost all your traveling by water. Dad says Kingston used to be the big market center for the area and people traveled there and back on the river."

The sun was warm and the air was humid. The smell of the wildflowers made me feel lazy, and I wanted to just sit in the meadow and watch the river flow by. I reminded myself that I had work to do, and I took out the notebook and pen I'd brought, although I wasn't sure just what I was going to write.

"Mom says you can tell there used to be an herb garden over by that wall," Karin said. "She knows all the wild herbs, even though they look like weeds. On a hot day you can smell them when you walk near there."

That's one of the things I like best about Belle Meadow. It always smells interesting and good with the herbs and the woods, especially when the magnolias are in bloom.

"Now, according to the map, the kitchen gardens must have been over near the herb gardens."

"Makes sense," I said, looking at the map again. "It seems to me that you wouldn't want to walk half an acre to get vegetables for supper."

"Tell me," said Karin. Every morning she had to go to the vegetable garden and pick the vegetables for dinner. "It's a real bother."

We both looked at the map carefully.

"It looks like most of the outbuildings were pretty close to the house, probably over there," I said, gesturing wildly to one side.

"Don't forget this place was pretty small, not like Mount Vernon with all of the gardens and outbuildings," Karin said. "By the way, the outbuildings were called offices."

"Where do you think the stables and things were?" I asked.

Karin pointed at the map. "Over by those woods, I think," she said. "It looks like there was a turnoff from the lane, or maybe a back road into the farm part. See, there's the lane coming from the main road up to the house. There's sort of a trail down there; let's go look at it more closely."

It wasn't too hard to tell where buildings or roads might have been, because most of Belle Meadow was either fields or

woods, and the fields weren't that close to the house. In the area where some of the old buildings and roads had been, the land looked different, not completely cleared but not completely wooded, either.

Part of the original lane was still used to get to the Martins' house from the road. The rest of the lane and the turnoff from the lane had become overgrown, but it wasn't hard to figure out where it had been. We followed the old lane for a while, then went back to the meadow.

"All right," said Karin. "If Alfred was talking about the tree from his study window, where would that have been?"

"Here's the house," I said. I was standing in the middle of the flat part. "I'm standing at the front of the house in the middle, facing the road."

The river was at my back, and I was facing roughly in the direction of the lane. The old overseer's house—the Martins' house now—was ahead and to my left. Beyond it were a few small sheds and some fields. To my right were the old woods and the filled-in clearings where the farm buildings might have stood.

"The problem's the angle," Karin said. "If Alfred was looking out his window at the back of the house, he was looking mostly at fields and the river. There aren't many trees there, except across the river."

I looked for a minute. "I never thought of that. Do you think that's what he meant? Or did there used to be trees in the fields?" I asked.

Karin looked at the map. "I can't tell for sure, but this looks like fields. And if you have fields you don't have trees."

"He must have seen something," I said. "He wasn't just imagining a tree."

"Maybe he was looking out the front of the house?" Karin suggested.

"All right," I said, turning around. "If I'm standing at the front of the house I'm looking at . . . millions of trees!" I groaned.

"We need an old tree," Karin reminded me.

I gave her a long look. "That's great, Karin. An old tree. An old sheltering tree. There can't be more than several hundred trees like that at Belle Meadow. And from the back of the house you can't see anything but fields and barns and things."

For a minute Karin was quiet, then she said, "Do you think this is hopeless?"

I thought a minute. "It just about is," I finally said. "The other day at the library I was looking at a book on old plantations. Most of them were bigger, but they all had similar plans, arranged just like they are today. The work rooms are in the back of the house, the living and relaxing part in the front. I think his library had to be in the back, more or less facing the river. People used their libraries for doing their work, not for sitting and reading."

I was beginning to get very discouraged. I tried to tell myself I'd known all along finding the treasure was a wild idea. If I'd come up with some clues about the specific location, we might have had a chance. But I hadn't. And there was always the question of whether the tree was still there after so many years. I suspected it probably wasn't, but I wasn't going to say that to Karin.

From the look on her face, I knew Karin had the same thoughts. Suddenly the afternoon sun didn't seem as bright.

"Let's explore the cemetery," I said, with more enthusiasm than I really felt. "We haven't done that for years. Maybe Alfred's buried there."

"All right," Karin said. "It's something to do, better than just standing here trying to figure out where some crazy person was sitting when he wrote his diary. Maybe we'll get an idea if we do something else."

As we were walking toward the graveyard Karin asked me, "Do you think we should get some help?"

"I don't know. Do you? We have Anne, and she's already come up with some ideas."

"I'm wondering if we should tell our parents. I think we could use some help," Karin said. "We aren't getting very far ourselves. But that's just the problem, would they help, or would they just laugh or smile and say 'that's nice, dear'?"

"There's Gary and Steve," I said.

"They might be in the laughing category," Karin said.

"They might not," I said. "Just the other day you were saying you and Gary never fight anymore and the two of you talk a lot more."

"He is getting a lot better," Karin said. "Maybe he's finally growing up."

I didn't remind her she was two years younger than Gary.

"I think Mom being so sick and now the money problem has really made a difference. I can't explain it, but it's like we're all in this together."

"Even Steve's changed," I said. "We've always been pretty good friends, though. He must have skipped that crummy stage. Maybe it has something to do with not having a dad all those years—it's always been just the three of us trying to manage. But even so, I don't want to say anything to them, not yet."

Karin nodded.

"I'll admit the whole idea of buried treasure sounds wild," I said, "but people do find things. And this could be pretty important for Belle Meadow."

The minute I said it I wished I hadn't. The sun got even less bright, although there still wasn't a cloud in the sky.

"I don't know, Karin," I said softly. "It would be great to find it ourselves without any help, but it might be a lot faster and easier if we had more people. But it's your diary and your treasure after all. Maybe you should decide."

"Maybe," Karin said.

Neither of us said anything.

"We could compromise," I suggested. "Let's try it ourselves for a month. We'll examine every possible tree on the place. After all, it has to be a tree that Alfred could see, so it's not in the middle of the woods somewhere. And there must be a few that are old and distinctive, and those would be the most likely. Then we could get some help doing the actual digging. And don't forget, Anne can help too."

"That's true," Karin said. "I don't mind Anne helping. I like her, even if you don't very much."

"But you know, I do," I said. "I finally figured it out Saturday when she got so upset because she thought I didn't trust her. We're not real close or anything, but it's been a lot more comfortable since then. And she's not droopy at all when you get to know her."

"A month, then," Karin said. "All right. Of course the tree might have died or blown down."

I didn't even want to think that such a horrible idea could be a possibility, but of course we had to consider it.

"We should look at every possible old tree that could have been seen from the house," I said. "And even if the tree isn't there we might find an old stump. I'm sure it would have been huge, and I bet they didn't dig it up. We might find some trace."

"I suppose we might," Karin said unenthusiastically.

"Let's start with the cemetery. I want to look at the gravestones now that I know who some of these people are."

"Tina, the genealogy expert," Karin said. "All right, but it seems as though the graveyard's on the wrong side from where his study would have been."

The old cemetery is at the edge of the woods where the trees are thinner. Just beyond the graveyard the woods get very thick, and in some places there's so much underbrush you can hardly walk through it.

"Cleared land must have been too valuable to use for cemeteries," I said, looking around.

"I guess so," Karin said. "Clearing that stuff," she waved towards the woods, "would be no joke." She sat down on part of the old stone wall that's still standing. "You know, I've always thought someday I'd like to restore this old cemetery. I'd put back the wall and set up the old stones. This is such a pretty place, even if it is a cemetery."

"It looks pretty good, even if it is a little run-down," I said.

"Oh, that's Dad," said Karin. "Every spring, even in the middle of all the plowing and planting, he clears the cemetery. We all help, but it takes a lot of time to trim around the old stones and the wall and the trees. It looks great when we're finished. Then he has Gary mow and trim it every so often through the summer to keep it up."

"Steve said he and Gary did the trimming last week," I said.

Karin was poking around the stones near the wall. "Here's my favorite," she called. "Meredith Graham. Isn't that a pretty name? She has a really elaborate stone with lots of carving and a long poem. And here's her brother—another Alfred, it looks like, or maybe Arthur. The Historical Society did a lot of work out here about five or six years ago, I think. It's good they did, because some of the stones are so faint you can't read them anymore. I wonder if you can restore stones like you can buildings, or if restoring ruins them. Look, here are the first Martins!"

"Here's one that just says 'daughter'," I said.

"Those are the sad ones, those and the babies' gravestones. There are a lot of those," Karin said.

"Is there a stone showing when the name changed back to Martin? You know, the Graham daughter who married her distant cousin?"

"I know the one you mean," Karin said. "Her stone's over in the far corner toward the river."

After looking for a few minutes, she showed me the stone: Elizabeth Graham Martin. I liked the name.

"You know, there are a lot of old trees right here," I said.

"There are a lot of old trees all over the place," Karin said, plainly more interested in the cemetery for the moment. "But they're all in the wrong place."

"Where's the right place?" I asked.

Karin thought a minute. "The one marked with a great big X carved on the trunk and a sign saying 'treasure here'!" She laughed, then got serious. "Did you bring the diary?" she asked.

"No, but I copied the sentence. 'May the whispering bough that has sheltered us so often protect us now. As I write this I see it from my window. May God be with us.'" I read. "Whispering tree—that doesn't tell us much."

"It tells us exactly nothing," Karin said. "Well, write down all the possible trees here. I'm going to look for the twins who lived into their nineties." She wandered off to the other side of the cemetery.

I was a little puzzled by Karin's attitude, but I knew it was her way of not getting upset about something. And I had to agree that the hopelessness of the treasure hunt was upsetting to think about.

I peered up at the various trees, then flipped through my small notebook and started writing. The cemetery was not only surrounded with big trees, it had a lot of trees within the walls. While I was writing down "big tree—north side of wall, halfway down," Karin hollered "Tina!" so loud my pen jumped off the page.

"What!" I said.

"The picnic area!"

"What?"

"On the other side of the cemetery—look, that funny cleared spot going toward the river. Dad says that used to be an old picnic area. And you always picnic under a tree in the summer!"

"Of course!" I said.

Karin started running across the cemetery.

Suddenly she gave a sharp cry, and I couldn't see her.

"Karin?"

"Here I am!" she called, but I still couldn't see her.

"Where?"

"Here!" I could see a hand waving in the air. I started across the cemetery. Even though it had been trimmed the week before, the undergrowth was thick enough that I had to go slow. I could barely see some of the stones and markers.

Karin was sitting on the ground, anxiously rubbing her ankle. "Be careful," she called, "don't trip like I did. I think I've killed my ankle. It hurts like anything."

I knelt down. "Do you think it's broken?" I asked. I didn't want to think about Karin out here with a broken ankle. It must be a mile from the house.

"No, it's just sprained or twisted. I'm sure it'll be all right in a minute." She sounded dubious, though.

"Shall I get your dad?" I asked.

"Heavens, no, don't get Dad. That'll just upset everyone. And anyway, we've got too much to do and I don't want anyone to think there's something wrong. It's starting to feel better already."

I didn't believe her, but I didn't want to sound discouraging, either. "Maybe you should put your foot up," I suggested.

"Good idea," Karin said, sticking her leg up in the air.

"Can you hobble over to the clearing?" I asked. "You could lie on the grass and prop your foot up on the wall."

I helped Karin stand up so she wouldn't put any weight on her ankle. She leaned on me and hopped to the wall, trying not to trip again on the uneven ground with its underbrush and protruding stone markers. She lay down and propped her foot on a section of the wall.

"How's that?" I asked.

"Not bad, aside from the fact I feel ridiculous. Are you sure this is what you're supposed to do? I really feel dumb lying here."

"I'm not positive," I had to admit, "but I think so. Even if this won't heal you instantly, it can't hurt."

"It can if someone walks by and sees me lying here," she said.

"Karin, who's going to walk by, for heaven's sake? This isn't exactly Main Street, you know."

"That's true. Look, why don't you look around some more for the tree. It might take a while before I feel like starting back, and there's no sense wasting the time. And look around for a sturdy walking stick while you're at it, all right?"

"I'll go back to marking down trees," I said.

I decided to walk around the perimeter of the cemetery and take my time. The cemetery was large: "A lot of dead people in the family in two hundred years," Karin had noted earlier.

It must have been a lovely spot at one time and had probably been cleared more than it is now. It wasn't hard to imagine how peaceful and lovely the area had been, with the clearing extending down to the river—the old picnic area. We'd have to look at that some other time, I decided.

I checked all the trees carefully, but no new ideas came to me. I found about a dozen trees that looked old enough. Finally I worked my way around to where Karin was lying on the ground. She was very still with her eyes closed.

"Karin!" I said sharply, hoping she wasn't unconscious.

She opened her eyes sleepily.

"Just resting," she said. "This is really very comfortable. I could take a nap."

"How's your ankle?" I asked.

"It must be better," she said. "I can hardly feel it."

"I have an idea," I said. "I don't think you should walk on your ankle. I could go get a wheelbarrow and . . ."

"I will *not* ride in a wheelbarrow!" she said, sitting up. "I'd rather crawl."

CHAPTER THIRTEEN

My Life Gets More Complicated

As it turned out Karin didn't ride home in a wheelbarrow, although I thought it was a great idea. I found a good sturdy stick in the woods, and she hobbled, limped, and hopped home. The porch steps were difficult. Just before we walked into the kitchen she straightened up, took a deep breath, and began walking almost naturally, announcing to her mother with a big smile, "Don't worry, it's not as bad as it looks," which is guaranteed to make a parent take notice.

What made it worse—although I'm not sure why—is that Mr. Neatherly was sitting at the kitchen table with Mrs. Martin, having a glass of lemonade. I felt guilty for no real reason.

"I think I twisted my ankle a little," Karin said to her mom.

"It looks to me like you twisted it a lot," her mom said. Even I could see it was swelling. "What on earth did you do?"

"I tripped over a gravestone in the cemetery," Karin said.

I could have kicked her for saying that in front of Mr. Neatherly.

"That graveyard is a hazard," Mrs. Martin said. "You're going to have to stay off your ankle for a while, and if it isn't better tonight I think the doctor had better look at it."

Karin made a face. "It'll be better tomorrow."

"I can work extra if it isn't," I said. I was thinking about all the guests arriving.

Mrs. Martin smiled and thanked me.

"I can pitch in," Mr. Neatherly said.

I couldn't picture Mr. Neatherly dusting, but it was a polite thing to say. "I waited tables in college, and I don't think I've forgotten how," he said.

"It's very kind of you to offer," Mrs. Martin said. "We'll just have to see how it goes. You need to get off your ankle," she said to Karin. I could tell by the look on Karin's face that her ankle was hurting, and I thought she probably should have ridden back to the house in a wheelbarrow.

"Mr. Neatherly has had an excellent idea," Mrs. Martin said to me. "He wants to talk to some of the old families in the area to see if they have any papers or letters that might relate to Belle Meadow. I suggested he might talk to your mother, since her family's been in the area for several generations."

"That's an interesting idea," I said, hoping I sounded more impressed than I was. I thought it was a terrible idea and would just give him an excuse to snoop. But then, I

reminded myself, he is a historian. "I don't know if she has any papers or not."

"I'd like to talk to her about anything she might have or any stories she might remember about the place. You never know what you'll find," he said. "Mrs. Martin tells me there are several people around whose families go back for generations."

By the time I'd ridden home he'd already called Mom and they'd arranged for him to come to the house tomorrow morning.

"I just don't like it," I told Anne. "I don't know why, but I don't like it."

"It was nice of him to offer to help if Karin can't work for a couple of days," she said.

"I know, he is nice," I said. "I don't think it makes any sense that I don't like him. I hope he doesn't know I don't, because then he might get secretive."

"People get secretive if they have something to hide," Anne said. "If he doesn't have anything to hide he'll just think you don't like him. By the way, if Karin can't work for a few days, why don't I work in her place? I'm sure Dad wouldn't mind if I missed a few days at his office, because this is kind of an emergency. And Mrs. McNair's not taking her vacation until August."

I never know what Anne's thinking. "That's really nice of you," I said, surprised. I knew if it had been me I wouldn't have thought of it. I just would have said to myself, "Oh, it's too bad about Karin's ankle," and that would have been that.

"Would you want to do that?" I asked. "It's not really much fun, you know."

"I know, but it could really help out, and they have all those guests coming. Why don't I call Dad and clear it with him?"

"All right," I said.

Of course everyone thought it was a terrific idea and Anne was a hero. I didn't mind. To my way of thinking, anyone who is willing to take on housework and dishes just to help out deserves to be a hero.

Mrs. Martin sounded relieved.

"She's depending on Karin a lot this summer," Mom told me. She and I were in the back garden trying to decide about vegetables for dinner. "For that matter she's depending on you quite a bit as well, but Karin's carrying the main load. The bed-and-breakfast wouldn't work at all without Karin and you. The fact that Anne can fill in makes a big difference."

"It sure does to me," I said. "It's thoughtful of her to offer. I'm not sure I would have, but then Anne thinks of things."

"You and Anne seem to be doing all right?" she said, in one of her half questions.

"Sure. It was a little tense at first, but it's fine now."

Mom was silent for a minute. Then she said, "There's a possibility she might live with us permanently."

"You mean forever?"

"More or less," Mom said.

"Does that mean we'd build an addition?" I said without thinking.

"Does that matter?" Mom asked.

I thought a minute. "No, it doesn't. We could use another closet, though. But why would she want to live here when she could live in Chicago? There's so much more to do there and all her friends are there. Do you think she likes it here? And what about her mom?"

Then I got it. "You're kidding," was all I could think of to say.

"Her mom thinks it might be a nice change for Anne," my mom said. Moms always say things like that.

"You mean she doesn't want Anne to live there? That's crummy."

"I don't think she means that," Mom said. "Her new husband travels a lot in his job, and she wants to be able to go with him. Nothing's been decided yet, but I wanted you to know there was a possibility."

"Well, I think Anne should live here then," I said.

"Are you saying that because you feel sorry for Anne or because you genuinely like her?" Mom said. "There's an important difference, and you need to be very clear about it."

"I know," I said. "I wouldn't want to live somewhere just because someone felt sorry for me." I thought for a minute. "Should I say something to Anne about wanting her to stay, or would it be better if I pretend I don't know?" I asked.

"I think it would be better not to say anything, at least at first. See what happens, and when the time seems right you could bring it up. Her mother called this morning and she and Walt talked a long time. Then Anne and Walt talked. Anne's a little upset about this, but she says she understands about her mom, and she's not too crazy about her new stepdad."

"I didn't even notice," I said. "I guess I was so worried about Karin's ankle."

"Anne seems to be a person who keeps a lot to herself," Mom said.

I agreed, remembering how she'd gone that whole first week thinking I hated her being here and never said a thing. Maybe I'll get more like Anne if she lives here. I don't keep much of anything to myself.

~⚜~

This morning Anne (on Mom's bike), Steve, and I biked out to Belle Meadow. Anne started right in serving breakfast, and you'd think she'd been waiting tables all her life. Mr. Neatherly smiled and said he guessed he'd been replaced before he even got started. Miss Groton just sniffed and changed her order to English muffins.

After our breakfast Anne and I cleaned the rooms for the new guests. Karin stayed downstairs on the sofa. "This is really dumb," she kept saying. "But I'm sure it'll be fine tomorrow."

Anne and Mrs. Martin and I just shook our heads. Karin's hopelessly stubborn at times.

Anne and I dusted and swept the guests' rooms. I took Miss Groton's (because it's harder) and Mrs. Hughes's rooms, and gave Anne Mr. Neatherly's and the hall.

Mr. Neatherly had already left for Allingham for his visit with Mom, so Anne could look around if she wanted. That may have been when she had her brilliant idea, which she told me about when we were biking home in the afternoon. Steve, as usual, had another hour of work to go.

"Listen," she said. "Didn't you tell me you thought there was something odd about Mr. Neatherly's books? I wouldn't know—you've met more historians than I have."

111

"Not really," I said. "But Karin's suspicious. I have to admit, though, talking to the old families is a good thing for him to do. Although it's not good if he finds out anything about the treasure."

"What's he going to find out?" Anne asked. We were riding slowly.

"I'm sure nobody knows about it, but I'm worried if he does get to look at some old papers he may find something."

"I hadn't thought of that. Well, I have an idea. He's a professor at some college, isn't he? This might be crazy, but why don't we call the college?"

I thought a minute. "Do you mean ask around about him? Do you think anybody would tell us anything?"

"No, not about him. I was thinking we could find out if he's even a professor. What if he's not? I could pretend I was thinking of coming to the college and majoring in history, and someone gave me his name."

I stopped my bike. "That's absolutely brilliant!" I said. "Would you do that?"

"Sure. If I can be an aspiring botanist, I can be an aspiring college student."

"It was all I could think of," I said. "Karin thought it was a great idea. After all, no one would believe it if I developed this sudden interest in botany, but no one knows you that well."

"I do have a pretty good cover that way," Anne admitted. "That works on the college part, too, although I absolutely am going to college, so it's not quite such a pretense as botanist."

"You might really like botany," I commented.

And to my surprise she said, quite seriously, "I think I just might. Anyway, when I call his college, if he's really a professor I won't have to talk to him because he's here. And if they refer me to someone else I'll just say I'm interested in colonial history and ask a few questions about the college. What have we got to lose?"

"I don't know what college he's from."

"Does Karin?" she asked.

"No, but she could find out."

"She can't ask him, though," Anne warned.

"Of course not," I agreed. "Let's call her the second we get home."

We rode the rest of the way home without saying anything. I couldn't tell if Anne was thinking about Belle Meadow or about living in Allingham for good. Her face doesn't give much away.

Karin had no idea what college he was from. "I think he wrote Dad a letter," she said. "I could look in his desk I suppose. Mom's upstairs resting."

While we waited for her to call back Anne practiced what she was going to say and I pretended I was the person who answered the phone at the college.

Karin called back in ten minutes. "We're in luck," she said. "It's Dorset College in Philadelphia."

Anne got the number from information and called, while I waited. I was nervous, but she was calm, which seemed backward to me. She went through her speech and answered a few questions. Mostly, though, she waited. Five minutes later she hung up.

"He's not on the faculty. They've never heard of him."

CHAPTER FOURTEEN

A Change in Plans

I thought about Mr. Neatherly all evening.

I really didn't know what to make of having learned Mr. Neatherly was a fake.

I'd asked Mom about his visit. He'd talked to her about her family and what stories she remembered hearing about the early days in Allingham. Then he'd asked her for suggestions of other people he might talk to. It all sounded like what a true researcher might do.

"We don't know for a fact he's fake," Karin pointed out the next day during one of our endless discussions about it. "In his letter he says he's affiliated with Dorset College."

"Did he ever say he was on the faculty?" Anne asked.

Karin thought hard. "I honestly don't know," she said. "I think he did, or else where would we have gotten the idea?"

"If someone says they're affiliated with Dorset College would you assume he was a professor there?" Anne asked.

And that was the question.

"I'm just going to ask," Anne said.

And to my astonishment, she did. She just walked up to him and announced that she was starting to think about colleges and where was he from.

What's more, she got away with it. She said a lot about what she might major in, and she wasn't sure, and she'd like a school that wasn't too far but wasn't too close either.

Anne's not that talkative, but she went on and on, and pretty soon she and Mr. Neatherly were talking about how to decide which college to go to. In the midst of all that talk—and there was a lot of talk—he said he was a professor at Dorset but that it was probably much farther away than she wanted to go.

"You're right," she said when he told her it was in Philadelphia. "I'd like one closer, where I could come home for weekends. Do you have any suggestions?"

He mentioned a few and she got a paper and pencil and carefully wrote their names down.

"I didn't want him to think I was interested in Dorset," she said later. "Now we know. He's fake."

I still had a lot of questions. Why was he here? Was he after the treasure? How did he know? Or, more important, what did he know?

I felt very restless when we got home.

Anne had a letter from her best friend who was on vacation in Oregon, and she went upstairs to read it. She'd told me that she and Natalie did everything together. I figured that leaving Natalie didn't make living in Allingham look any better. I thought she probably had a lot on her mind, and

I wanted to leave her alone. I decided to sit out in the backyard with a glass of lemonade and read, but then I remembered I'd finished my last library book two days ago.

I poked my head into the sewing room. "Mom, I'm going to the library," I announced.

"Oh, good," she said. "Would you pick up a book for me? Mrs. Wessels is holding it at the desk. I told her I'd be over this afternoon, but Mrs. Albright called and she's coming over."

All the more reason to go to the library, I thought. "I'll be back in time to help with dinner."

The library in Allingham is bigger than a person might expect for such a tiny town, but a lot of people in the county use it too. Mrs. Wessels had been the librarian forever, and she knew what everyone read.

"Here's the book your Mom wanted," she said handing me a book. "And here's one that just came back that I think she'd like. You can check them out with your books."

"Thanks," I said, taking the books, one a memoir of some general and the other a novel. Mom read everything she could find on the Civil War, fiction and nonfiction. I bet she knows as much as some historians do about it. The thought made me think of Mr. Neatherly again.

I wondered if I was reading the situation all wrong. He might have very good reasons for pretending he was with Dorset College. Maybe he was going to be on the faculty there, or just wanted to be. Wasn't I being awfully suspicious for no reason? Lots of people tell lies, for all sorts of reasons. And, what was the harm in this case? Obviously if he was lying *that* was wrong—I could still hear my grandmother on the subject—but he could have very good reasons I didn't know about.

The mystery shelves looked bare and picked over, but I managed to find one I hadn't read in a long time and couldn't remember how it ended. None of the books on the new-books shelf appealed to me, so I wandered over to the section on Virginia. I decided I needed a good picture book to look at, not the kind for little kids but the ones with lots of photos and illustrations. I particularly like the ones on different places. There's nothing like a good picture book for getting distracted when you want to be. I always check out at least one.

The first title that caught my eye was *A History of Virginia Plantations*. I wasn't sure I really wanted to spend more of my spare time on plantations, but the book looked thick and it was loaded with pictures. Besides, it occurred to me that Anne might like to look at it.

I took the book back to the table where I'd left Mom's books.

The pictures were interesting, and the book seemed to spend time on the point that not all of the plantations had been the large, famous ones. For once an intelligent book on plantations, I thought. I checked to see if there was anything about Belle Meadow.

Sure enough, there it was in the index! But when I turned to the page there was barely a sentence on Belle Meadow "outside of Allingham." All it said was that many of the smaller, less-well-known plantations were fertile ground for more work and archaeology.

"I already know that," I muttered to myself. Still, I'd have to tell Karin that Belle Meadow is mentioned in the book.

Certainly our house wasn't mentioned. Of course, we don't live on a plantation. But our house is never mentioned in books on old houses in Virginia, and there are a lot of those books. You'd think someone would have said something.

But then, how could someone mention it? The place didn't have a name, and all anyone could say is "the house at 47 Plummer Street." For that matter, it isn't even "the Mueller house" anymore since Mom married Dad. For them it's become "the Westcott house," but for Steve and me it's still "the Mueller house." Did that mean that now it was "the Mueller-Westcott house?" I couldn't see anyone writing *that* up in a book.

I decided the house needed a name. Instead of changing my name, I probably ought to be thinking of naming our house. I wasn't sure why anyone would want to put our house in a book, at least not yet. My grandmother had lived there, but the house doesn't have much history. Even though it's old, it isn't old like Belle Meadow. Still, if I got famous, it would be useful for people who write my biography if I lived in a house with a name. I decided I needed to think about this point.

I flipped through the pages, admiring the pictures and wondering what the houses would look like inside. One picture in particular caught my eye. The house wasn't very large and it was situated on a small river, like Belle Meadow. It was called Charlton Point. I decided to read about it to see if it said anything about the house.

A few minutes later I sat up straight. "That's it!" I said out loud.

Mrs. Wessels looked at me. Fortunately there were only two other people in the library.

"Sorry," I said. "I just found the answer to something I've been wondering about." I could feel my face was very red.

Mrs. Wessels must be used to people making wondrous discoveries in her library, because she didn't say anything except, "That's always an event!" and she smiled.

I read the paragraphs again, slowly.

Until the time of the fire, the river provided the main source of transportation to Charlton Point. Not only was most of the business of the plantation conducted by using the river, but much of the visiting and social life was carried out by river. The roads that existed were barely more than trails or rough lanes in many places. Travel by the river was more comfortable and often faster. And while the boats weren't very big, they could transport more than the small carts which were all that could manage on the so-called roads.

Gradually the roads improved, however. As towns began to grow up, the land became more settled away from the rivers and streams. This pattern became well established throughout the more rural areas of Virginia.

The fire at Charlton Point occurred in 1815 or 1816. It apparently damaged the main house enough to require some major rebuilding, but it would seem that the house wasn't totally destroyed. In fact, it appears that a substantial portion remained to be used in the "new" house.

When Charlton Point was rebuilt, however, the orientation of the house was changed to reflect the changes that had taken place with the roads. Where the "old" house had faced the river, the "new" house now faced the road. Since the river was still heavily used, both for commerce and for visiting, the side of the house facing the river, now the back of the house, still had a commodious porch and receiving hall.

I read the paragraphs again, but instead of "Charlton Point," I was reading "Belle Meadow."

All along Karin and I had thought the house had faced the road, and the back of the house had looked out over the farm buildings and fields.

But what if the house had faced the river! Apparently many houses did in those days. Look at Charlton Point. The difference was that after its fire, Charlton Point had been re-built and more or less turned around. Belle Meadow had burned completely, and the family had simply relocated to the overseer's house. If Belle Meadow had been rebuilt, it too might have been reversed so the house would face the road.

How odd that both places had fires, I thought, but then I remembered fire had been a common hazard in the days of open fireplaces. It seemed to me several of the old planta-tions we've visited had fires at some time or another. I de-cided it wasn't strange after all.

I closed my eyes and pictured myself back in the meadow, standing where the old house had been. Only this time, in-stead of facing the road as we thought the house had, I was facing the river. If the study was at the back of the house, I thought, it's looking away from the river. I mentally turned around so my back was toward the river.

I remembered the house had been angled toward the river. If the study was in the corner at my left, it looked toward the farm buildings and the fields. But if the study was at the corner to my right—that's where it was!—that's it!—the study faced the picnic area and the graveyard.

I knew as sure as I was sitting there in the Allingham Carnegie Library that Alfred Graham had been looking toward the graveyard and the picnic area when he'd written the entry in his diary.

And I remembered something else from our explorations the other day. In my mind's eye I could see Karin lying in the grassy area with her foot propped up against the crumbling wall, shaded by a tree with a big knob where a great limb had once been.

That's it! That's it! And the noise from the breeze, a sort of rustle—I hadn't paid any attention to it because of Karin's dumb ankle. No, if it hadn't been for her dumb ankle I wouldn't know about *that* tree at all!

I checked out my books, raced out of the library, threw the books into the basket, and biked home as fast as I could.

CHAPTER FIFTEEN

Plots—of Land and People

I was so excited I called Karin right after dinner. I figured if I talked in code it wouldn't matter who might be listening.

"I know where it is!" I said, when she was on the phone. "Listen! I found this book and it was talking about the houses facing the river and then they turned and I know where the you-know-what is!"

"What are you talking about?" Karin asked.

"You know," I said. "The you-know-what."

"I know the you-know-what," Karin said, sounding a little exasperated, "but I don't know the other part about the river turning. And what book?"

"Listen," I said, and I read her the paragraphs. There was a lot of static on the line, and I had to talk more loudly than I wanted to. After I finished Karin didn't say anything. I got a little frustrated and forgot all about talking in code.

"Remember in the cemetery when you were lying on the ground going to sleep while I was trudging around in the heat looking? That's where it is!"

"I was not going to sleep, I was prostrate with pain," Karin said. "And it wasn't even hot."

"Never mind that, think about the tree. It's perfect. I know that's the one. And if the wind's just right like it was the other day, you can hear it rustling through the leaves."

"There's probably not a spot on the whole place where the wind doesn't rustle through the leaves," Karin said. "That's what wind does in wooded areas, you know."

"Anyway, I heard it and it didn't sound like regular wind and leaves. And, the tree was one of those I put down on my list of suspects. That's where the you-know-what is!"

There was a long silence.

"Karin," I said, "think of who's buried there. Someone's family."

"Oh," Karin said. "Of course! That's what he meant by the sheltering part. That's probably more important than the tree, you know."

I nodded, and then realized she couldn't see me. "Of course! That's it! Now, how are we going to do this?"

"Beats me."

"Karin!"

"All right. How about tomorrow afternoon?"

I looked around to see if anyone was there. "What about Anne?" I whispered. I could hear her downstairs talking to Steve about the Cubs.

"Why not?" Karin said. "She's already in on it. You know, if we do this it's going to be a lot of work. She can help. Of course, being a sensible person, she may not want to spend a hot sweaty afternoon digging for you-know-what that isn't even there. I need to go now. Talk tomorrow."

She hung up, and I thought I heard a second click, but there was a lot of static, too.

Anne was all for the plans. "I've never dug for a treasure before," she said, managing to sound enthusiastic. "Of course I'll help. Show me on the map where you think it's buried."

We pored over the map.

"Why don't I just redraw this?" said Anne. "I'll put the house in facing the river." She took out her sketchpad from the desk. "Tell me everything you can remember about where things may have been. Now, where was the tree?"

She sketched quickly, and the map began to take shape.

"It makes sense that the tree would be between the old picnic area and the graveyard. Sounds very sheltering to me. And there's not going to be many trees in the cemetery, so it probably would be on the outside. Were there any stumps?"

"I wasn't looking for any, but there are some here and there near the wall."

"So even if it isn't exactly the tree, we know about where to dig," Anne said. "Sheltering the graves of his parents and brother and sister is really important. What does Karin think?"

I shook my head. "I think she wants it to be there, but she's trying to pretend that she doesn't care. You should hear her."

"I can understand that," Anne said. "It's hard to want something a lot, and she must feel strongly about all the problems with Belle Meadow. When you want something too much it hurts a lot when you can't get it."

~⌘~

I woke up the next morning with a stomachache: nervous, most likely. It was almost as bad as when I'd had the small part in the school play this spring. I knew my five lines perfectly, but I kept getting more nervous until the day of the performance when all I could think about was wanting it to be over.

At breakfast Mrs. Hughes announced her appointment in Kingston had been cancelled.

"How could it be cancelled when she hasn't gotten a phone call or anything?" Karin whispered to Anne and me in the kitchen.

"Maybe she called," I said.

"Come to think of it she used the phone right after I finished talking to you last night. But then she calls her husband pretty often," Karin said.

The three of us just looked at each other, then Mrs. Martin told us to carry out the muffins and eggs while they were still hot, and we had to get busy.

All morning I kept telling myself there was nothing to be nervous about. After all, if the treasure wasn't there, what was the worst that could happen? I'd be very disappointed, and so would Karin, but what would be the harm?

I didn't really believe all hope for saving Belle Meadow would be lost if we didn't find the treasure. But I knew finding the treasure would be bound to help. I kept telling myself there was absolutely no reason to get myself into a state about digging for treasure this afternoon.

My stomach wasn't listening to my head, though, and it kept getting queasier and queasier. I could hardly bear to watch everyone eat.

Karin's ankle was a lot better, and since the doctor had wrapped it she could move around more easily. Even so, she still was favoring it a little. She was able to help more than she had been, though, and the three of us got through the morning work quickly. The four new guests left after breakfast for a day of sightseeing.

Right after lunch Miss Groton took her crocheting out onto the porch, and Mr. Neatherly left to go into Allingham. Steve, Gary, and Mr. Martin were working in one of the fields across the road, on the other side of the house from where we would be.

It seemed like a perfect setting for digging, until I went out to pick vegetables for dinner and saw Mrs. Hughes sitting on the porch facing the meadow and graveyard. She had a lot of antique magazines and catalogs spread around her on the sofa, but you didn't have to be much of a detective to tell that she wasn't looking at them.

I told Anne and Karin as soon as I got back to the kitchen.

"We'll just have to be extra careful," said Karin. "If we go out the north door and circle around the woods, she won't notice us. And what if she does? She can't really see anything from the porch."

Anne and Karin raced through the dishes while I snapped about five hundred beans for dinner. Finally we were through.

"Don't act too secretive," Karin said. "We'll look suspicious."

"There certainly isn't anything suspicious about sneaking out the north door and going down the lane and through the woods to get to the graveyard on the opposite side," I remarked. But I knew Karin was right and I decided to pretend I was looking for rare wildflowers to add to the collection I don't have.

"We should actually start in the meadow again," Karin suggested. "But I still think we should sneak through the woods and get there from the other side."

I wanted to go right to the cemetery and start digging, but I knew that starting in the meadow was the best idea. We had to be very sure since we couldn't very well dig up the whole graveyard—and what an awful thought anyway.

"Did you bring everything?" Karin asked as we started out.

I nodded. "When we get to the meadow I'll show you the new map Anne drew of how the house might have looked and where the study might have been. It's really neat."

"I had Tina tell me every single detail she could remember from the other day," Anne said. I knew she was pleased with the map.

Between Karin's ankle and our route it seemed to take a long time to get to the meadow. We showed Anne where the house was supposed to have stood. She walked around the area very carefully. Every few minutes she'd stop and look toward the fields and woods, as if she were looking out of an imaginary window.

"It makes a big difference to know the house was facing the river," she remarked. "Look at the difference in what you see if this is the back of the house instead of the front."

"I think that's the key to the whole thing," I said, modestly. "But wait until you see the tree! I think that's the one," I pointed, "see, right by the wall between the picnic area and the graveyard, toward the river."

"It does stand out a little, so Alfred could have noticed it from his window," Anne agreed. "Let's go look at it."

A few minutes later we were standing under the tree. "Now, look at that great big knot where a limb must have been cut off or fallen!" I said.

"It's pretty high up, all right," Karin remarked. "It certainly could have been a 'sheltering' limb."

"This looks like a good place to me," Anne said.

We stood around for a few minutes, looking at the other trees. None of us wanted to say "let's start digging." Even I was reluctant. It was such a big step, and what if we were wrong? We'd never talked about the actual digging part.

Finally Karin remarked, "There are shovels in the toolshed."

"All right," I said.

Then we remembered Mrs. Hughes on the porch. "No, wait," Karin said. "The shed is too close to the house. Dad keeps some tools in the barn. Let's try there first."

I tried not to think about having to explain why we were carrying shovels in the middle of a warm Saturday afternoon. "Digging up treasure" didn't sound like it would be a good explanation at all.

"Let's cut back through the woods and go in the back of the barn," Karin suggested. She was still hobbling, but it didn't slow her down. "Her ankle's really going to hurt tomorrow after all this," I told myself.

The barn was dark, and it took a few minutes for our eyes to adjust to the lack of light.

"The tools are in a little room off here." Karin found the light switch. We could see a workbench piled with tools, and more tools were hanging from nails and hooks in the wall. There were only two shovels, but we decided that was enough.

"Just a minute," I said when we were ready to start out.

I walked through the barn and looked out one of the windows facing the house. Even from the distance, I could tell Mrs. Hughes was no longer on the porch. She was wearing a red skirt, and I would have seen that bright spot of color on the sofa.

We left the barn, and Karin and I each carried a shovel. Karin tried to use hers as a crutch, but she stumbled and almost fell. After that Anne and I carried the two shovels, holding them in front of us so that if anyone saw us they might not notice what we were carrying. It was awkward, and we were relieved to get into the woods.

"We did that pretty well," I commented. "We would be good spies."

We decided to start digging close to the tree and directly under the knob from the old bough.

"Won't we run into roots?" Karin asked.

"I don't know. Maybe," I said. "If we do, we'll dig somewhere else."

For a minute the three of us just stood.

"I guess we might as well start," Karin said.

"You start," Anne said. "It's your land. You can do the official groundbreaking."

It turned out that "groundbreaking" was the right word. The ground was really hard. After twenty minutes our digging had barely made a dent. After an hour we were all sweating and puffing, even though we'd been taking turns digging and resting. But at least we had a definite hole.

"How far down do you think we should dig?"

"I don't know. They couldn't have had time to bury it very deep, or at least I don't think so."

"Wouldn't it be deeper now?" Karin asked. "When the archaeologists were here I remember them saying that sometimes when a place gets overgrown more soil accumulates on the ground, so anything buried in the ground would be deeper than it was originally. That's why the old house foundation is buried now."

I groaned.

"Maybe some spots erode," Anne suggested hopefully.

It seemed like we dug forever. Everything hurt. My back hurt, my arms hurt, even my toes were beginning to hurt. Then suddenly Anne jabbed her shovel into the hole and hollered, "I've hit something!"

I leaped up from where I was resting against the wall.

"Maybe it's a root or a rock or something," I said, trying not to get too excited.

"No, I've really hit something!"

All of us knelt down and started scraping the dirt with our hands.

"This isn't a root or a rock! I'm sure of it! Look!"

Karin had scraped around the edge of a strangely shaped something. She was right. It wasn't a rock or a root. It was the corner of a moldy case of some sort.

"Oh, my gosh," I said, and sat back to look. I could hardly believe there actually was something in the hole.

Karin was too stunned to speak.

Anne stood up, stiff from crouching.

"HEY!" she shouted suddenly.

Karin and I looked up, startled.

I saw a splash of red.

CHAPTER SIXTEEN

We Take to the Woods

Just then out of the corner of my eye, I saw a man in the corner of the clearing. He was backing into the woods so he wouldn't be seen.

I knew in a flash who it was, and I started running after him, with Karin and Anne right behind me. For someone who had strained her ankle a few days before, Karin kept up a fast pace.

"I bet he's parked in the lane—the old one," Karin panted. "There's a path that leads . . . we can cut through the woods . . . beat him. . . ."

The path was overgrown. There was no telling when it had last been used, but it was a path and it was still better than floundering through the woods. We could hear the man trying to run.

At first the path led away from the noise, but it suddenly turned and we were on an old dirt trail in front of the man.

We could just glimpse a dark car parked at the end of the trail.

"I'll get the car!" Karin said. "You get him!"

Anne stopped suddenly. We could hear the man coming toward us, stumbling through the underbrush. A moment later he was running more evenly.

"He's on the path!" Anne whispered, and started looking around frantically.

"Here!" I picked up a long, thick stick.

"He's going to be coming along here," I said. "This is where the opening is, and he should head right for it. Let's get him then."

Anne nodded and crouched behind a bush at the edge of the opening. I did the same.

"We'll listen, and if it sounds like he's not coming out here, we'll have to move," I whispered. "But if he does . . ."

I made a jabbing motion close to the ground.

"Trip him?" Anne whispered.

I nodded.

We could hear the man now; he was very near. It sounded like he was trying to hurry but wasn't having much luck, because he made a great crashing racket. A minute later he broke out of the denser part of the woods and started down the path-like opening.

Mr. Neatherly! Just as I had suspected. Spying on us! After *our* treasure!

I've never been so furious in my life. I could feel the rage boiling up inside me. I made myself concentrate on his running. If the timing were wrong, my plan wouldn't work. I could feel Anne's tension beside me.

Suddenly he was there, running in smooth even strides. Just when he was almost in front of us, I thrust the heavy stick into his path. He went down in a heap.

With a yell Anne leaped out from behind the bush and sat down on his back. A split second later I did the same, and Mr. Neatherly was under us, squirming and jerking, but unable to move.

We started yelling for Karin.

"Over here! Get help!"

Karin came running up. "I let the air out of all four tires. Can you hold him? I'll get Dad." And before we could answer she raced away, hobbling at an incredible rate.

"Dad!" We could hear her calling in the distance. "Dad!"

Mr. Neatherly suddenly was still.

"Listen," he said. "This is unnecessary. Let's talk."

"No chance," I said.

"You've got the wrong idea," he said. "Let me up and we can talk about it."

"No."

Anne looked around and quietly picked up a rock.

"I'd just lie there quietly if I were you," a familiar-sounding voice said, but in a stern tone I'd never heard before.

I almost fell off of Mr. Neatherly when I saw Mrs. Hughes standing in the path ahead of us. Then I remembered the glimpse of red I'd seen just before I spotted Mr. Neatherly trying to get away.

"Even if you could run away it wouldn't do you any good," she said.

Anne and I looked at each other. Neither of us knew what to say.

It seemed like hours before we heard someone starting into the woods.

"Tina! Anne!"

"Over here!"

"We've still got him!"

Mr. Neatherly groaned.

A minute later I was relieved to see Mr. Martin with Gary and Steve. They hauled Mr. Neatherly to his feet and started walking him back to the house. The fight seemed to have gone out of him, and he walked quietly and dejectedly. Anne and I followed, with Mrs. Hughes trailing after us. I knew I ought to say something to her, but I didn't have the faintest idea what to say.

When we got to the yard Mr. Martin told Mr. Neatherly to sit down on a lawn chair. Mr. Neatherly sat.

"The girls say you were trespassing and spying on them," he said sternly.

"They don't know what they're talking about," Mr. Neatherly said. "Why would I spy on them? They're crazy."

"We are not!" Anne said.

She had the same look on her face that she'd had when she thought I was hiding the diary from her.

"You spied on Tina! You think there's something hidden, and you want to *steal* it. You're just a crook!" she said, furious but with a cold calm.

"Something hidden out here?" Mr. Martin said. "What about it?"

I decided it was time.

"Buried treasure!" I announced.

Just then the sheriff's car stopped in front of the house, and the sheriff and another man got out.

"Who called the sheriff?" Steve asked.

"I called," Mrs. Martin said. "When Karin raced past the house yelling about a thief and a trespasser—well, I decided to ask John to drive out. Karin doesn't exaggerate."

"I understand you're having a problem with a trespasser?" the sheriff said. "Bob Neatherly?"

"That's right," said Mr. Martin.

"I'm doing my research," Mr. Neatherly said with as much dignity as he could muster.

"We'd better talk this over," said the sheriff. "Just what happened today?"

"I was walking the site," said Mr. Neatherly.

"He was spying on us," said Karin.

"It sounds to me like he sure took off when you saw him," said Mr. Martin.

"What would you do with the three of them chasing you and yelling like maniacs?" Mr. Neatherly demanded.

"The question wouldn't have even come up if you hadn't been spying on them," Mrs. Martin said. "And what's this about spying on Tina?"

I could feel my face get very red.

"The day I found the secret compartment in the table, someone was in the hall watching me. I found something else, too, and whoever it was saw it. The thing I found said something about what we're looking for this afternoon. How would Mr. Neatherly even know to spy on us this afternoon if he didn't know about the diary I found earlier? And the only way he could know was by spying on me earlier. He probably listened on the phone last night, too." It had dawned on me that Mr. Neatherly must have known what we were planning.

Mrs. Hughes broke in unexpectedly. "He *was* listening," she said. "I saw him. That's why I decided to cancel my appointment today and stick around. I've known something was going on. Someone's been prowling around in the house at night, for one thing. And odd things, like someone using my boots. Last night after I saw Mr. Neatherly here listening in on Karin's conversation, I thought I'd keep my eye on things today."

Mr. Martin turned to Mr. Neatherly.

"How about it?" he asked, but Mr. Neatherly didn't say anything.

Anne nudged me. "Dorset College," she hissed.

"Ask him where he's from," I said.

Everyone turned to Mr. Neatherly, but he still didn't say anything.

"He says he's from Dorset College, but when we called, they hadn't ever heard of him," Anne said.

"We have some talking to do," said the sheriff. "Where's your car? I'm going to follow you back to town and we're going directly to my office."

"It's in the old lane in the back of the woods," Karin volunteered. "But I let the air out of the tires."

"Good going, Sis!" Gary said, grinning.

The sheriff's car, with Mr. Neatherly in it, had barely started out of the lane when everyone turned to us.

"What's this about buried treasure?"

"You found a diary?"

"There was an old diary and it talked about a buried treasure and we found it! It's buried in the graveyard! Let's go look!" Everyone except Mrs. Hughes took off running, even Mrs. Martin, who's a pretty good runner.

While I was running I thought, "What if it isn't there? What if we just imagined it?" But I could still see the brown corner sticking up out of the hole.

We had to wait for Karin, who was hobbling badly after all the running she'd done. She must have had the same thought, because as she came up she called out, "Is it still there?"

"Yes," I said, "just where we left it."

We all peered into the hole.

"There's something there all right, and it looks like it's been there a long time," Steve said.

CHAPTER SEVENTEEN

The Treasure Is Revealed

"There might not be anything in it," I said, suddenly feeling very nervous. It was one thing to dig up a trunk with just the three of us, but with the whole family looking on the disappointment would be too horrible if it were empty.

Gary grabbed a shovel and started digging around the corner of the box. We all watched him, and no one said a word. Anne moved over and put her hand on my shoulder, as if she knew what I was thinking.

"Please let it be all right," I kept saying to myself. "Let there be something, even if it's not much."

Finally Gary could grasp an end.

"I think we can get it now," Steve said, carefully shoveling dirt away from the other end.

The box—at least what I could see of it—did look like a small trunk. It was dirty brown and looked moldy, and there seemed to be a leather casing of some sort around it.

"It weighs a ton," Gary said, as he and Steve heaved it out of the hole and onto the ground.

We were very quiet while Gary undid the straps holding the casing in place. The old cracked leather fell away, and underneath was a trunk that looked like it was in about the same condition as the casing.

"Oh!" someone said. I didn't know if it was me or someone else. I felt as if I were holding my breath.

"Is it locked?" Mrs. Martin asked.

"I don't think so."

Gary fumbled with the clasp. There was a sharp click. He pushed against the lid, and although it moved a little, it didn't open.

"Here, let me try," Mr. Martin said. He rapped sharply against the sides of the trunk and tried the lid again. This time it opened stiffly.

We all moved forward to get a look. There seemed to be dozens of cloth packets of all sizes.

"Tina?" Mr. Martin said. "I think you're the moving force in all this. . . ." he stepped aside.

I took a deep breath, reached for one of the smaller packets and carefully unfolded the cloth. When the last fold fell away, I was holding a large brooch, a deep red stone surrounded by a gold mounting. I didn't know what to say. I looked up, and looked at everyone in turn. "Is it real?" I finally asked.

"I don't know," Mr. Martin said, and his voice sounded strange. Mrs. Martin looked like she was going to cry.

It was Anne who came to the rescue when nobody seemed to know what to say. "Isn't that just beautiful?" she said.

"Look at the red lights in the stone! Tina, Karin, you did it! You found the treasure! I'm so proud of you!" And she hugged both of us.

Then everyone was hugging and laughing and talking. Mrs. Martin reached for another packet and began to open it, and suddenly all of us started opening the packets as fast as we could.

"Look at this!"

"I've got silver!"

"Have you ever seen anything like this?"

"It's a treasure! It really is a treasure!" Karin kept saying, and I kept answering, "I see! I see! It really is!"

Anne just stood and beamed at everyone, admiring each thing that was unwrapped.

The assortment was stunning. Many of the pieces were silver, including a set of small silver bowls with intricate etching. It was very tarnished, but you could still see the detailed workmanship and graceful lines.

"I think we'd better take this back to the house," Mr. Martin said finally.

"I'll get a wheelbarrow," Gary said, and ran to the toolshed.

"I want to hear the whole story!" Mrs. Martin said while we waited. "The very second we get back to the house, I want to hear everything!"

"Can I call Mom?" I asked.

"Tell her that she and Walt should come right out!" Mr. Martin said, and I ran ahead to the house.

Mom and Dad came while we were still laying everything out on the large dining room table.

Mrs. Hughes had disappeared upstairs, but Mrs. Martin went to get her. "You're in on this too!" she said.

I hoped I would remember later to thank Mrs. Hughes for looking out for us.

None of us could take our eyes off the table. There were all types of silver pieces—bowls, cups, candlesticks, even a tray. In every odd corner of the trunk there had been small packets that contained jewelry, either made up into pieces or just gemstones. One package contained rough-looking pebbles. Mr. Martin thought they might be uncut gems.

"This must be very valuable, I would think," Mom said, gesturing toward the table.

"I would think so," Dad said.

Mr. and Mrs. Martin looked at each other, and I knew what they were thinking. Belle Meadow won't have any more money problems.

"I think everything's going to be all right," Mr. Martin said.

That broke the spell. Suddenly, everyone was talking and laughing and hugging each other with an incredible feeling of relief and celebration. As long as I live I will never forget the feeling of happiness that suddenly swept through all of us.

"Now, tell us," everyone demanded when we'd calmed down a little. "Don't leave anything out."

I thought a minute. "It all started with the table that day. Remember the papers I found? Well, there was a diary, too." And I told about finding the diary and everything that had happened since. I tried to emphasize the fact that I knew the diary wasn't mine to keep, and that I wouldn't have kept it very long anyway, because I felt a little guilty about that.

But nobody seemed to be interested in my ethical dilemma, so I just went on with the story.

When I came to the part about how I thought someone had spied on me from the hallway, and how I decided later it had been Mr. Neatherly because of his interest in Belle Meadow, Mr. Martin nodded. I told how Karin and I thought he didn't have the right kind of books for a historian, and he nodded some more. He must have wondered about Mr. Neatherly, too.

Miss Groton gave a start when I said something about the books.

"My family is one of the oldest in the area," she said. "My ancestors lived five miles from Belle Meadow for more than a hundred years, and Mr. Neatherly never once asked me about it. I don't think he even found it out—and he should have. He was just all wrong as a historian. But continue telling us about the treasure."

I was so interested in what she'd said that for a minute I forgot where I was in my story. Then I remembered. "It seemed like a really crazy idea at first, but then nothing we found said the treasure wasn't here, so we decided to keep on with it. We didn't have anything to lose, especially if we didn't say anything to anyone. And then when we knew the old house had probably faced the river, well, that had to be it," I concluded.

"I'd like to see the diary sometime," Mrs. Martin said.

"Oh," I said, very embarrassed. "Of course, it's *yours!*"

"You were very clever to get all that information and figure out where the treasure might have been hidden," Mrs. Martin said, smiling.

"We all worked on it together," I said, "Karin and Anne and me."

"And Mrs. Hughes helped us at the end." I hoped she hadn't guessed how suspicious we were of her.

She smiled at me. "But you're the ones who figured out the mystery and that Mr. Neatherly was a fake."

"Well," said Dad, "it sounds like the three of you sure took care of Mr. Neatherly. He didn't have a chance with all of you after him this afternoon. I would love to have seen you tripping him and then leaping on top of him. The man probably didn't know what hit him!"

CHAPTER EIGHTEEN

Aftermath

When Bob Neatherly found out the Martins were considering pressing charges for trespassing, even though he was officially a boarder at Belle Meadow, he finally talked about what he'd been doing. He admitted he'd been in our house, looking for the diary. He'd worn Mrs. Hughes's boots, so that if anyone noticed tracks or anything, the suspicion might fall on her.

"The nerve!" Mrs. Hughes was indignant when Mr. Martin told her.

Several days later, Mr. and Mrs. Martin and their lawyer talked to Mr. Neatherly in the sheriff's office. Even though Karin, Anne, and I weren't there, we learned from the Martins what had been said.

"At first I didn't know there was a diary," Mr. Neatherly said, "but I guessed there was something important hidden in that table. I'd seen Tina take something out of the compartment, and when nobody said anything about it, I didn't know if I'd been mistaken or if she was keeping something back."

"Did you find the mention of the table in the old will?"

"Sure."

"But how did you know in the first place there was something hidden?"

"I came across another diary from this area, a later one. It mentions Belle Meadow pretty often. It also mentions a story about the people at Belle Meadow burying some valuables before they fled. From what I could learn, it didn't seem to me that anyone had ever found the buried items, so I thought I'd look. I figured it would be easy. I wasn't going to keep the treasure, you know. I just wanted to find it."

"Oh?" Mrs. Martin said. "You were going to *give* it to us? I don't believe you."

"Don't you see," Mr. Neatherly said, "I needed to make a big find, so I could get a good job as a historian. I've always wanted to be a famous historian, and I figured this was my big chance."

"Your bigger chance was to put in some good, hard work," Mr. Martin said. Then he and Mrs. Martin turned their backs and left without saying another word.

~⚬✦⚬~

Things never really got back to normal during the summer. Karin and I kept working at the bed-and-breakfast, which was a great success. I never really liked my job very much, but I didn't mind it either.

Steve kept working at Belle Meadow, too, and he seemed to like it better. "Everyone's in a pretty good mood all the time, and I'll be in great shape for football," he said one day when we were biking to work.

Mom's sewing business kept expanding, and Anne sometimes helped her with the hems and easy parts. Mom paid her, but I'm not sure even with pay I'd sew.

Anne continued to work at Dad's office several mornings a week. She gradually met some other kids, and all in all, she seemed more relaxed about being in Allingham.

Late in the summer the Martins invited all of us to Belle Meadow for a celebration dinner. Even the weather cooperated. There was a slightly cool feel in the air; you could tell fall might be coming. The boarders had agreed to go out for the evening, and there weren't any other guests.

And what a celebration it was, complete with Mrs. Martin's plum wine. Even Karin and I got a glass with a microscopic amount of wine in the bottom.

When we were all sitting down at the table Mr. Martin stood up. "I want to propose a toast," he said. "To perseverance, especially on the part of Karin and Tina."

I blushed.

"We have something . . ." he continued, and he handed me a small package.

"Shall I open it?" I asked, which sounded dumb, but I didn't know what to say.

"If you like," Mrs. Martin said.

I felt very clumsy with everyone watching. Finally I unwrapped a small square box.

Inside was a silver pendant of delicate filigree surrounding a small red stone. The chain was very fine. Even when I'd first seen it, tarnished and dim from being neglected for so long, I'd thought it was just beautiful.

"Oh!" I looked at Mom, wondering if it was all right to accept such a beautiful gift. Mom nodded slightly. "Thank you very much . . . it's just beautiful . . . I'll really treasure it. Thank you!"

"She'll treasure the treasure," Steve remarked, and everyone groaned.

"We have something of our own to celebrate," Mom said. "We have a new member in our family. Anne's going to be with us this winter!"

Everyone cheered, even though it wasn't really news to anyone.

Anne turned as red as the stone in my necklace, but I could tell she was pleased.

"Yes," she said, "now I can take botany!"

I don't think anyone knew just why Karin and Anne and I thought that was so funny, but everyone smiled politely.

"It's pretty nice to have a sister!" I said. "This is going to be a good year!" And I meant it.

Two momentous things happened that fall. The tree fell during a terrible thunderstorm with a loud scary crash. We were all stunned, and for days we kept asking each other what if it had happened a year earlier? It still gives me goose bumps to think of it.

The second thing was that Anne took botany and liked it. Thank goodness.